A Baker's Dozen

Thirteen Short Stories

Gene Masters

Published by Escarpment Press

Introduction

Here are thirteen short stories written over the past few years as the spirit moved me. An idea might come at an odd time, stew in my mind for a while, and I would have to set it down on paper. It would not be nearly enough for a novel, but would be an interesting story anyway—at least to me. I would come back to it later, revise, add, subtract.

One can easily tell from the mix of subjects, and the eclectic subject matter, that my mind works in strange ways. There's my history—decades-old history, now—in diesel-electric submarines, coupled with my fascination with all things military. This is contrasted with my conviction that war, however apparently valid the cause, is the ultimate expression of mankind's utter stupidity.

Where the rest of these stories came from, I cannot say: a man sentenced to crucifixion for a minor offense; a person who cannot quite glimpse the ghosts pursuing him; a mob hit gone sour; some social commentary; and other weird happenings.

These are thirteen stories that I consider my most interesting. I do so hope you agree.

Gene Masters
Knoxville, Tennessee
Summer, 2023

Table of Contents

Socialism ………………………………………………………………1

The Bridge………………………………………………………… 9

Just Business …...……………………………………………………17

Crossing the Line …………………………………………..…..27

The Crucifixion …………………………………………………...33

The Tide of War …………………………………………………39

The Shadow People …………………………………………...…..47

Ghost Boat …………………………………………………...…...55

The Queue …………………………………………………...…..69

Marking Time …………………………………………………...75

Survival …………………………………………………………81

The Night Visitor …………………………………………………89

The Cavern …………………………………………………...…..95

Socialism

Dan Wilcox came home with his family that evening after a day and night in the mountains in their travel trailer, only to find a family of four making itself at home in his living room.

"Who are you?" he demanded, "and how did you get in here?"

"Easy, Dan. It is Dan, isn't it? The letters in your mailbox were addressed to a Daniel Wilcox. We're the Folger family. I'm Charlies, this is my wife Margaret, and my kids, Billy and Judy. We got in through your back door. You really should keep it locked, you know."

Dan was sure he had locked the back door when they left that morning, but let that slide for the moment. "And what exactly are you doing here, Mr. Folger, is it?"

"Yes, Folger. Charlie Folger. Why Dan, we live here now."

"You what?"

"We live here."

"That's impossible. *We* live here—me, my wife, my two kids. *We* live here."

"Of course, you do, Dan, of course you do! But this *is* a big house, and there's plenty of room for all of us, wouldn't you say?"

"No, I wouldn't say. Now I'll thank you if you and your family would just pack up your stuff, and leave this house immediately!"

"But Dan," Charlie replied in a soft voice, "how can we do that? Where would we go? You certainly wouldn't want us to sleep out on the street, now, would you?"

Dan thought for a moment. Then he said, as firmly as he could, "That is none of my affair. This is *our* house, *not* yours, and *we* live here. Where *you* go, and what *you* do is just not *my* problem!"

"Oh, Dan," Charlie said, disappointment dripping from his lips, "aren't you a Christian?"

"I am. We are," Dan answered proudly. "We attend the United Christian Church, Fundamental, on Laurel Street — Pastor Conklin."

"And would putting us out on the street be the Christian thing to do?"

"I don't know what the Christian thing to do might be, Mr. Fowler, but I do know about civil law. And the law says you have no right to invade my — *our* home. You have no right to be here. Please leave, now, all of you, or I'm going to call the police."

"I don't know how to explain this to you in any other way, Dan. Do what you must, but we can't leave. This has to be our house as well as yours, because we have nowhere else to go."

Dan took out his phone and called the sheriff's Department. He explained the situation to the person who answered the phone, a Deputy Shaw.

"These people," asked Shaw, "are they threatening you or your family in any way?"

"Well, no. But they don't belong here."

"Possibly not, but are you in any danger?"

"Well, no. At least not yet, we're not."

"Tell you what, Mr. Wilcox, the Department is really short-staffed right now, but we'll get a deputy out there as soon as we can."

Disappointed, Dan thanked the deputy and hung up the phone.

"They're sending a deputy out as soon as they can," he said to Charlie, "then you'll *have* to leave."

Charlie grinned. "Okay, Dan, we'll just stay till he gets here, okay? So, meanwhile, what's for dinner? Me, my wife, and kids haven't eaten all day, and we're pretty hungry."

In desperation, Dan looked over at his wife, and rolled his eyes. Susan Wilcox just shrugged, and said, "I'll see what I can whip up."

No sheriff's deputy showed up that evening, and when bedtime arrived, the Folgers produced sleeping bags, and set them out on the floor of the living room. Billy and Judy each had their own; Charlie and Margaret were cuddled together in a larger, single one. The TV was in the living room, and while the rest of the Wilcox family was upstairs in bed, Dan, a night owl, was watching the late comedy show with the sound turned down. He had just settled down in his recliner, when Charlie said, "Dan, do you mind? Me and the kids are trying to sleep."

"What?"

"The TV, Dan, it's keeping us awake."

"But I turned the sound all the way down."

"I know you did, Dan, and we appreciate that, really. But the flickering screen and even the muted dialogue is keeping us awake."

Dan looked over at the Folger children, and they were obviously sound asleep. "Oh, all right," he finally said. He turned off the TV and left the room to go upstairs to bed.

"Good night, Dan," Charlie called after Dan, as he was mounting the stairs.

THE NEXT MORNING WAS A school morning, and Susan Wilcox was busy getting their children, Meghan and Max, ready for school, while Charlie was still upstairs, dressing to go to work. It was only when Susan set breakfast out that the Folgers got out of their sleeping bags in the living room, and, still in their pajamas, came into the kitchen dining area and sat at the table.

"Smells yummy," Charlie said. "Nothing like the aroma of frying bacon and the smell of fresh coffee to wake a body up in the morning." He then he started singing a jingle: "The best part of waking up . . ." he began, and then laughed. "Folgers! The coffee people you know? No relation, unfortunately!"

Nonplussed, Susan set out four more plates and put some more bacon into the frying pan. When Dan came down to breakfast, the four Folgers were sitting with Meghan and Max at the kitchen table. There was no room left for him, and the coffee was all gone. He ate a breakfast of two strips of bacon, toast, and orange juice, standing up at the kitchen counter.

Charlie had just left the house with Meghan and Max to walk them to the school bus stop, when Susan asked Margaret, "Your children are still in their pajamas. Aren't they going to school?"

"Oh no," Margaret replied. "I home school them."

"Oh," Susan said, uncomfortable with the idea that the Folger children would be underfoot for the entire day. "Well. Okay, then," she finally said.

With the Wilcox children now safely on their way to school, Dan returned home to kiss Susan goodbye, pick up his briefcase, and then drive off to work. He found the Folgers camped out again in his living room — all four still in their pajamas. Benny and Judy were atop their sleeping bags, playing on the floor, while Charlie and Margaret, cuddling on the couch, watched the morning TV news show.

"Don't you have to go to work, Charlie?" Dan asked.

"Oh no, Dan," Charlie replied. "I can't work. I'm on full disability."

Dan frowned, and, in response, Charlie said, "Oh, and by the way, I told Social Security to start sending my disability check here. I hope you don't mind."

Dan was too furious to answer. Fuming, he left the room, grabbed his briefcase, pecked Susan on the cheek, and then drove off to work.

DAN CALLED THE SHERIFF'S DEPARTMENT again that day, and was again told that they would get a deputy out to the house as soon as they could.

When he arrived home after work, Dan asked Susan if she had heard anything from the sheriff. When she said that she hadn't, Dan was forced to form a desperate plan to at least get the Folgers out of his living room.

Dan put Billy Folger in with his own son, Max, Judy in with his daughter Meghan, and Charlie and Margaret into the guest room.

"I told you, Dan," Charlie said, before shutting the door to the guest room, "this house has plenty of room."

But when Dan went down to the living room to catch some TV before bedtime, he found the four children ensconced in front of the set, watching a rerun of "Frosty the Snowman."

"Aren't they adorable?" Susan opined. "The four of them get along so well!"

All Dan could think about was the football game that was on, on another channel. Disgruntled, he went upstairs to bed. Fortunately, he managed to fall sleep, and was still out when Susan finally came up to bed.

The next morning, determined to be rid of the Folgers, Dan skipped work and went down to the county court house, looking to file the papers necessary to begin the eviction process.

"To file the eviction papers, you will need to show us a copy of your deed to the property, the last three months' paid utility bills, proof of payment of last year's property taxes, and your marriage license," the clerk told him.

Dan spent the rest of morning gathering up the necessary paperwork, and filed the eviction papers late that very afternoon.

"How long will it take before the eviction notice comes through?" Dan asked.

"We're running pretty far behind, Mr. Wilcox," the clerk said, "but not more than a month or two."

Dan left the county court house fuming, but still determined to see the last of the Folgers.

TWO MONTHS PASSED, AND THE two families had actually fallen into the semblance of a daily routine that, when observed from the outside, would have convinced an onlooker that they managed to live together in a kind of peaceful coexistence.

Then the eviction papers finally arrived.

Dan immediately brought them down to the sheriff's headquarters, saw the sheriff himself, and demanded that the papers be served. The sheriff agreed to serve the papers that very afternoon. Dan was elated at the prospect that the Folgers would be out of his house by the time he returned home from work.

But when he did return home from work that day, he found Susan, Meghan, and Max, and all their personal belongings sitting out in the front yard. Max was reading a comic book, Susan was furious, and Meghan was crying.

"What have you done?" Susan asked.

"I've had the sheriff serve eviction papers on the Folgers," Dan replied.

"But the Sheriff evicted *us!*" Susan exclaimed. "He served the eviction papers on us!"

"There's been some mistake," Dan said. But when he went to enter the house, the door was locked, and his key no longer opened the door. He could hear the Folgers talking and moving around inside, and banged loudly on the door with his fist, but no one answered.

The Wilcox family moved into the travel trailer. "Just for the night," Dan promised. "We'll straighten this out in the morning."

But in the travel trailer the Wilcox family stayed. Dan was unable to straighten out the mix-up with the eviction process. Despite his passionate pleas to the sheriff, who claimed that his men had done just as the court had ordered, Charles and Margaret Folger were now in complete and undisputed possession of his house.

Eventually, both families adjusted to the situation. The Folgers lived in the house, and the Wilcox family lived in the travel trailer parked in the front yard. Every weekday morning, Dan walked Meghan and Max to the school bus stop, kissed Susan goodbye, and drove off to work. And every month, when the mortgage payment came due, Dan Wilcox faithfully paid it.

The Bridge

Vanya climbed into the cockpit of his jet—the plane he called his *Dytyna*, or baby—an aircraft that was actually older than he was. Vanya always thought the familiar cockpit was made just for him; and it fit him like a glove. He knew every gauge, instrument, and switch. He knew their foibles, which dials he could rely on, and which he might have to tap a time or two to move its needle.

He settled in his seat and pressed the button that would slide the canopy bubble closed. As usual, the bubble needed some help: a hand to start the slide in motion. Once it was locked in place, with the green canopy light on, Vanya signaled his crew chief on the tarmac below that *Dytyna* was ready for flight.

The weather was only marginal. The dawn sky was overcast, and rain threatened. Not ideal for his regular mission—that of ground troop support—Vanya mused, but perfect for this one. No matter. Vanya had flown his *Dytyna* in all sorts of weather.

The crew chief pulled the wheel chocks free as Vanya stepped hard on the brakes. He switched on the engine, listening to the turbine wind up, felt the airframe vibrate, and his baby come to life. Once the engine stabilized, Vanya nodded to his crew chief, standing below on the tarmac, that he was ready to move. The man stepped clear of the aircraft, signaling his understanding. Vanya taxied into position, and again stood on the brakes. Once the aircraft settled into its thrust stabilization setting, Vanya pushed the throttle forward, released the brakes, and the aircraft leapt forward. *Dytyna* practically jumped up into the sky.

Vanya brought his plane up to fifteen hundred meters and steadied off. He checked all his instruments, and everything looked to be in order. His radar was on, and the scan showed that the surrounding skies were empty. That was, Vanya knew, somewhat deceptive, and tended to give one a false sense of security. The enemy flew more modern aircraft, and their radar was far superior. On a good day, his aircraft's radar could detect another aircraft at one hundred fifty kilometers; the enemy radar could detect his plane at two hundred twenty. This meant that the enemy could detect him, and launch an air-to-air missile at him, before Vanya even knew there was someone else in the air.

He had checked the two British-made cruise missiles locked in their pods prior to takeoff, and now his weapons panel showed that they were both ready to deploy. Vanya turned the aircraft toward enemy occupied territory. Once he approached the battlefront, he would be bringing *Dytyna* down to ground level. There he planned to stay, under enemy ground-based radar, and practically undetectable to air-based radar. Vanya would stay there until the mission was complete, and he had returned to more-or-less friendly airspace—*if* he returned.

His mission was simple. All Vanya had to do was blow up a bridge. Except that this was just not any bridge. This was *the* bridge. The main enemy supply lines crossed this bridge. Without it, the enemy battalions would soon become bereft of food, fuel, and ammunition. And the enemy was not stupid. The enemy defended this bridge with his best ground-based defense systems: radars, missile-launchers, rockets, and by continuously flying combat air patrols.

Simple. Vanya had to just bring his plane into position, at the seacoast, just one hundred sixty kilometers from his base, and release the missiles. The air-to-ground cruise missiles would then fly over water for the remaining hundred sixty kilometers, skimming the surface by just two meters, only to rise up at the last minute to destroy the target. Simple. Just fly those one hundred sixty kilometers at tree-top level, over enemy-occupied territory, brimming with ground-to-air missile systems, and patrolled by enemy aircraft.

Trouble started almost as soon as Vanya entered enemy controlled territory. He was hugging the terrain as was the plan, flying just thirty meters from the ground, subsonic at five hundred knots. It took every bit of his skill, and even a momentary lapse in concentration could cost him the mission, not to mention his life.

The radar detection system light suddenly came on, then immediately went out. About thirty seconds passed. Then it came on again, and went off again. Somewhere ahead, an enemy ground defense radar operator was getting an intermittent signal, and was struggling to lock on to his target — struggling to lock on to *Dytyna*.

Then the missile warning light lit and the alarm sounded. Vanya guessed that the ground defense system operator had decided to launch anyway, aiming a missile in the dark, bargaining that the missile would find its target in flight, lock on it, and destroy it.

The operator's radar, after all, was limited by the earth's curvature; its depression angle, how far it could look down at a target, was limited. The missile itself, although initially radar guided, was not limited by the earth's curvature once in flight; its guidance system could search out and lock on its target independently. Still, ground clutter or a release of aluminum confetti from the target aircraft, could confuse it, throwing the missile off target. Knowing this, and looking to save his supply of confetti, Vanya headed for the nearest clump of trees, flying low enough so that the tree tops occasionally scraped the belly of his aircraft. He could only hope to lose the missile in the clutter before the forest ran out.

When the missile warning light did go out, he breathed more easily. Somewhere behind him, the missile ran out of fuel and exploded, with any luck, Vanya thought, over some enemy encampment. The very idea brought a smile to his face. He turned *Dytyna* back on a course to the seacoast and toward the bridge.

Vanya returned to his ground skimming. Occasionally, his radar, looking forward, would pick up something in front of him higher than thirty meters off the ground. Still flying subsonic, at just five hundred knots, there was nonetheless precious little time to react to some structure closing in ahead, or even an occasional hilltop.

Vanya was almost fifty kilometers away from the seacoast, when his radar suddenly showed an airborne intruder inbound and closing fast. Seconds later, his radar detection system lit up again, this time with the system solidly locked on. This was no ground-based radar. Another aircraft had detected him, probably outside his own radar range, vectored in on him, and then shut off his radar until he was almost on top of *Dytyna*.

Vanya was expecting a missile warning light next, but none came. Vanya was still weighing his options, when suddenly an enemy jet fighter screamed by overhead and close, followed by a stream of 30mm shells and a sonic shock wave. Luckily for Vanya, the fighter's pilot had overestimated *Dytyna's* speed, and the shells passed harmlessly in front of his plane. As the intruder climbed to avoid running into his own shells, Vanya put his aircraft into a steep climb as well, veering off to the right at full throttle. Vanya couldn't match his adversary's twin engines for power and speed, nor its superior mobility, but he could at least get out of his cannon range.

Once he reached fifteen hundred meters, Vanya leveled his *Dytyna* off, and backed off on the throttle, maintaining a barely subsonic six hundred fifty knots. He searched the sky with his radar, but could find nothing. But his radar detection system was still lit; that meant that the enemy fighter was still out there, and locked on him, but past his own radar range. That was not good. It meant that a missile could already be coming his way, released from that still undetectable source.

But when no missile warning light lit, and no alarm sounded, Vanya was nonplussed.

Why had the enemy pilot not launched a missile against him? He quickly thought through the inventory of missiles and other armament that the enemy was capable of deploying. Certainly, this fighter *could* deploy air-to-air missiles, and the enemy usually equipped them with a mixture of air-to-ground missiles and a variety of guided bombs.

But the enemy always arrogantly assumed air superiority, and usually equipped its fighters in a ground-support role. They relied on ground-based air defense systems to take out any flying intruders. Of course! The reason the fighter had attacked with cannon fire was that the missiles it carried were totally unsuited for air-to-air combat! The only weapon he *could* use against *Dytyna* was his cannon!

What to do? Vanya could not stay at this altitude and avoid detection by ground-based defense systems, bound to proliferate now, as he approached the seacoast. But if he returned to the treetops, then he could not see the enemy fighter approach at supersonic speed, again in time to avoid another strafing run. Suddenly, he was forced to decide — and fast — as a second radar locked in on him: this time a ground-defense unit. There was nothing for it now, but back to the treetops. Seconds later, he was back at thirty meters altitude, but now still running at six hundred fifty knots, again headed toward the seacoast. The only good news was that the ground-based radar had lost him. The bad news was that the fighter's radar had not, and was still locked on him.

Now, Vanya needed to fly high enough so that his own radar could detect his adversary, but still low enough to remain undetected by a ground system. But how high was high enough, yet not too high? Was there some "sweet spot?"

Vanya increased his altitude to fifty meters. The air ballet he had danced with the enemy jet had brought him no closer to the coast, and it still was fifty kilometers away. But, at his current airspeed, that was only thirteen minutes flight time. If he could only maintain course for thirteen more minutes! But not three minutes passed before a ground-based radar locked in on him. It was at that same moment when the enemy jet chose to come in for another strafing run, and it was closing fast. Vanya slowed to five hundred knots, and returned to the treetops, thinking perhaps he could make the enemy plane overshoot him again. Not this time. As 30mm shells ripped into her fuselage, *Dytyna* shuddered, violated, but continued flying. She shook again as the shock wave passed. Vanya scanned the dials in front of him. Nothing seemed out of order, but that did not necessarily mean that no fatal damage had occurred.

Vanya was now less than forty kilometers from the coast, and he knew that he could not risk surviving another strafing run; he must launch his missiles now, or blow the mission.

Vanya pushed the throttle forward, put *Dytyna* into a steep climb, and went supersonic as he leveled off at two thousand meters. Ground-based radar locked in on him just as he released the port missile, and then the starboard. Each lit off in turn, fell away from the aircraft, and, dropping to the treetops, headed toward its target.

With the missiles gone, *Dytyna* was suddenly twenty-six hundred kilos lighter. The enemy jet was closing again, and *Dytyna's* missile warning light lit and the alarm sounded.

Vanya turned toward the incoming jet, turning left as tightly as he could, and headed back to the treetops. This put his exhaust toward the incoming missile, and Vanya released a cloud of chaff. The enemy jet easily maneuvered left to keep *Dytyna* in front of him, and quickly released another hail of bullets, which passed harmlessly over *Dytyna*. As the enemy passed through the chaff, the incoming missile hit him head on, and his jet exploded.

Vanya slowed to six hundred knots, settled back at thirty meters altitude, and headed *Dytyna* home.

THE FOLLOWING MORNING, THE ENEMY'S official news agency issued a report that partisan saboteurs had attacked the bridge with a hail of six, shoulder-fired missiles, four of which were intercepted by the enemy's missile defense systems. Unfortunately, two missiles had evaded their air defenses, and both spans of the bridge had suffered minor damage.

Satellite photographs, however, later showed that both spans of the bridge had been breached. The damage was extensive, and would probably take months to repair.

Just Business

Angelo waited for his friend to come home. Getting into Henry's townhouse was easy; the security system was Walmart basic, easily overcome. *You'd think that someone with as much B&E experience as Henry would know better,* but Angelo figured that it was just another case of the "cobbler's kid wearing the crappiest shoes in town." Angelo chuckled at the thought. His Grandma used to say shit like that all the time. The old lady was gone years and years ago—when he was still a kid—but he still recalled her fondly.

It had been dark out for a very long time, and it was well past midnight when Henry finally showed up. Henry famously did not drive, and took cabs everywhere. It was pretty obvious, then, when his taxi pulled up in front of Henry's place. Angelo watched through the front door sidelight, as Henry paid off the cabbie and the taxi took off.

Angelo backed well off from the door. He heard Henry turn his key, first in the door handle lock, then in the bolt lock, and then push the door open. He stepped inside the hallway, onto the sheet of plastic Angelo had spread out on the floor. Angelo could hear him mumble "What the . . ." when the alarm system didn't announce the opening of the front door with a ring tone.

Angelo watched in slight amusement as Henry closed the front door behind him and flipped up the cover on the keypad mounted next to the door. In the light of the outside porch light, Angelo saw the perplexed look on Henry's face when the keypad remained unlit.

"It's a cheap-shit system you got there, Hen. Bypassing it was a piece of cake. You could afford better."

You had to give Henry credit. He didn't even flinch when he heard Angelo speak to him out of the darkness of his living room. "Well, Angelo," he said, "most of the yahoos in this neighborhood know well enough to steer clear of this particular house."

"Ya think?" Angelo asked.

"I do," Henry replied. "I got a reputation. They know better than to mess with somebody what's connected."

"Well, Hen," Angelo agreed, "you are definitely connected. Maybe *too* connected."

"Yeah. All right, Angelo. You ain't just paying your old buddy a friendly visit. I suppose Betto sent you here. I thought he and I had straightened all that shit out. That we had come to an understanding."

"Apparently not. Otherwise, he wouldn't have sent me, yeah?"

"Guess not. But he really had no reason to. We coulda worked all this out. Shit! I thought we had!"

"And I guess you thought wrong, Hen."

"Shit, Angelo, come on. You can't do this. You're my friend. How long we known each other? Geez — since we was kids! Why you? You can't do this, Angelo."

"Nothing personal, Hen. You know it's just business. You, of all people, should understand that. Besides, Betto didn't give me much choice. Maybe that's why it was me he sent. Figured maybe you'd put up less of stink if it was me. You and me having known each other so long, and all."

"Maybe. But you still can't—"

The silenced Beretta still had a loud bark in those confined quarters. First, one in the head. The red blotch appeared so quickly on Henry's forehead that his eyes, still wide open, never had time to register any surprise. His body slumped back against the front door. Angelo snapped two more off, this time into Henry's heart, as his body slid down to the floor, slid down onto the plastic sheeting Angelo has placed on the hallway floor two hours earlier.

Angelo was a professional. The 9mm hollow-point bullets he had used were charged with just enough gunpowder to enter Henry's body, but not to exit. Much cleaner that way. No blood and brains splattered all over the place—much less bleeding altogether. Angelo waited a bit. Equipped with the silencer, the Beretta had made minimal noise, but even so, three gunshots might still be heard by a neighbor, and nosy neighbors tended to call 911 when they heard gunshots. He didn't have to worry about any errant blood spatter, either. Betto said he didn't care if the cops found Henry's blood in the house, but Angelo would rather they didn't find the body there. Better they never found it altogether, he figured.

An hour later, and still no cops, Angelo wrapped Henry's body in the plastic sheeting, making a clean package that he secured with duct tape. Henry wasn't a big man, maybe one-eighty at most, but that was way more than Angelo could carry in a dead lift. But Henry had obligingly placed a runner carpet in the hallway, and, with Henry's body on the runner, he could grab one end of it and drag him through the house, and then to the back door.

Angelo left the place via the back door, the same way he had entered. Looking left and right, and seeing no one, he stepped out into the chill night air. No moon that night, and that was good. The alley was otherwise dimly lit: just one street light at either end, and a neighbor's porch night, about three houses down. He had parked his white Ford Envoy panel van in the alley back there, right up close to the building, and as much out of sight as possible. But now he backed it up parallel to Henry's back door.

There wasn't much in the alley. Opposite Henry's place, a wooden fence ran the entire length of the property. The scant backyard was paved only wide enough for a single car, and so, it was mostly used for garbage cans and such. Angelo worried that someone might come out of one of the neighboring houses to take out the trash or something, but there wasn't much he could do about it if they did. Such activity was unlikely at this hour, anyway.

Getting the body into the back of the van was near impossible. Dragging it out the back door and into the alley was easy enough, but getting it up into the van was a nightmare, even using the metal ramp that attached to the van's rear bumper, what with all that dead weight. By the time he was able to close the van's rear doors, Angelo was soaked through his clothes with sweat; but Henry's body was safely stowed, and nobody had entered the alley to observe his labors.

Then, he went back up into Henry's house, and made sure the front door was relocked and all the lights were out. He could relock the back door, but there wasn't much he could do about restoring the alarm system. Still, there was no sense in making things any easier for the cops to figure out, so he had worn gloves, and, as far as he knew how, had left no fingerprints or DNA behind.

He started up the van and began to drive slowly out of the alley.

Suddenly, there were bright, blue-tinted headlights blocking the alleyway; a car had turned into the alley and was heading in his direction. "What the . . ." he said aloud, cursing the sudden glitch that had just appeared in front of him. To make matters worse, the idiot had just started to lean on his horn. *That rat-bastard will wake up the entire neighborhood. That's all I need!* Thinking quickly, Angelo began to slowly back up the van, yielding ground to the new arrival. The driver of the oncoming car, sensing victory, stopped sounding his horn, and instead revved his engine, as he claimed the ground that he had demanded.

Angelo had almost backed completely out of the alley, when a man appeared behind the van, a man suddenly lit up by the vehicle's backup lights. He was an elderly person, unshaven, a shock of wild white hair, black suspenders and grey undershirt suddenly visible in the rearview mirror.

Angelo then saw that the oncoming car had stopped, headlights still blazing, just behind the house next to

Henry's. Its door now swung open, loud rap music filling the night air. It was dislodging passengers: young people, obviously "under the influence."

There was a rap on Angelo's window. Angelo looked left and saw that the old man who had been behind him, was now next to the van, signaling that he should roll down his window. Reluctantly, Angelo lowered the window.

"Damn kids!" the old man said. "No respect for anyone. It's the middle of the night and the bastards are making enough noise to wake up the dead!"

I hope not, Angelo caught himself thinking, but said instead, "Yeah. Look, I don't want any trouble. I'm just trying to drive out of this alley, so I can go home."

"Yeah. Okay. But what you doin' in this alley anyway? Not exactly a regular thoroughfare, now, is it? It's the middle of the night, too. What *are* you doin' here?"

Angelo thought quickly. "Visiting an old friend. We had just said goodnight, and I was just going home."

"Yeah? Old friend, is it? And who might that be?"

"Henry. Henry Messina."

The old man's expression suddenly changed, from a look of confrontation to one of fear. "Oh," he said. "In that case, don't let me stop you."

"Sure thing," Angelo said, and backed the rest of the way out of the alley, before he raised the window back up and took off down the street, heading toward the desert.

IT WAS ALMOST DAWN BY the time Angelo finished burying Henry. Admittedly, Angelo hadn't dug the grave very deep, but, in all honesty, he just wasn't as young as he used to be, and the desert gets really cold at night. He buried the Beretta with Henry, silencer and all, and the rest of the ammo he had prepared for the hit. It was a waste of a perfectly good piece, but the last thing he wanted to do was to be found in possession of an untraceable gun used in a murder. Dirty and exhausted, he drove home, and slept through most of the day.

IT WASN'T TWO WEEKS LATER when the cops came around: two uniforms and a guy in a cheap suit, a detective who flashed his badge. "We know you're a colleague of one Henry Messina," the detective said, "and this morning a local citizen prospecting with a metal detector out in the desert got a hit. The hit turned out to be a pistol, and the pistol turned out to be buried next to the body of your friend Henry."

Angelo did his best to register surprise at the news.

"Seems Henry must have crossed one of your other business colleagues. This was a mob hit, Angelo. One to the head and two to the chest. You might not know anything about that, now, would you?"

"No, officers, nothing at all."

"Figured you might say that. How about you take a little trip with us downtown?"

"Sure thing, detective, right after I call my lawyer."

"You can do that downtown," the detective said, and cuffed him.

Downtown, in one of those sterile interrogation rooms that they have in all police headquarters, Angelo cooled his heels for an hour waiting for his lawyer to show up. The guy Betto sent looked like some kid straight out of law school. "Who are you?" Angelo asked.

"Vincent Carillo. My aunt Wilma is Mr. O'Reilly's wife."

Geez! *The mook is Betto's wife's nephew!* Angelo thought.

The detective who had come to his door then came into the interrogation room and identified himself as one Detective Jerome Chubb, LVPD. The name fit him better than his clothes, since he was short and round. "Angelo," he said, "the medical examiner says Henry's been deceased twelve days. Puts his death sometime the night of the twelfth. Were you in town that day?"

"Can't be sure. What day was that?"

"Tuesday."

"Tuesday the twelfth. Let's see. Yeah, I think I was in town that day. Usually am, during the week. I gotta work you know."

"Yeah, we know all about your work. Betto O'Reilly's company, Waste Systems Management, isn't it?"

"Yeah. I'm Recycling Manager."

"I'll bet you are," Chubb said. "What we really want to know, Angelo, is where you were in the early morning hours last Tuesday, say one or two in the morning?"

Angelo glanced at his lawyer. The kid gave him a blank look back. *Big help the mook's gonna be.* "Pretty sure I was home in bed, Detective, like I am most nights at that hour."

"Really?" Chubb said. "'Cept we got a witness that picked your mug shot out as the guy driving a white Ford van outside of Messina's house that night."

Angelo didn't say anything. Neither did his lawyer

Chubb continued. "The crime lab can't say for certain that's where Henry Messina was offed—in his house—but the ME did fix the date and approximate time of death. And right about that time, a taxi dropped Henry off at his house. So, it's pretty certain that Messina was killed there, and that the job was done neat and clean—by a professional."

Chubb paused for effect. He looked hard at Angelo, and said, "That witness places you at the crime scene, Angelo, right about the time Henry Messina got hit."

Angelo looked at his lawyer. "Ain't you gonna say anything?" The kid just looked back at him and swallowed hard. Angelo looked back at Chubb. "Shit," he said, "What I want is a real lawyer."

"Don't know as I can help you with that, Angelo," Chubb answered, "but I probably can help you if you tell us who ordered the hit."

"I need some time to process all this," Angelo replied. Then to the lawyer, he said, "You make sure you go tell Betto I'm thinking about that, will you kid?"

"Yes, sir," Carillo answered.

Later, in his cell, Angelo realized those were the only two words the kid had said during the whole interview.

The kid, meanwhile, had reported in to his uncle, filling him in on exactly how Angelo's interrogation had gone down. "The cop said they got a witness, Vinny?" Betto asked.

"Yeah, Uncle Betto. One that places Angelo at the scene of the crime. I checked. The witness is solid. Says he saw Angelo up close — talked with him, even."

"Crap. That tears it. Angelo blew this whole thing. So now we can't let Angelo get us into any deep shit. We just can't."

What you gonna do, Uncle Betto?"

"Never you mind. No need to get you involved any further than you already are. I'll take care of it from here. This is just business, Vinny. You understand? Nothing personal, just business."

Carillo wasn't quite sure he liked the sound of that, but he didn't say anything in response.

THE NEXT MORNING, ANGELO WAS found hanged in his cell. His jailors said that they had checked on him about midnight, and then, again at four in the morning, and he was just fine. It was when they were bringing him breakfast, that they had found him. Nobody could say for sure where the shoelaces that were used had come from. The sergeant who checked him into the jail was sure he had collected Angelo's shoelaces, but there were none in the envelope containing his personals. The ME still concluded that Angelo had died by suicide.

Crossing the Line

Fifteen days after leaving the submarine base at Pearl, our boat, *Orca*, arrived at the sea routes north of New Guinea in the Bismarck Sea, and the Japanese stronghold at Rabaul. None of the time in transit had been wasted. Lieutenant Commander Jake Lawlor, our skipper, continued to hold emergency drills, at least one daily, keeping the crew razor sharp.

But during the two days before they arrived on station, the crew of *Orca* not actually on watch, was devoted entirely to nonsense. That was only because the boat would be crossing the Equator: zero degrees of latitude, the imaginary line that divides the planet in two, separating the northern and southern hemispheres.

It was traditional in all the maritime services to especially commemorate all the first-time passages of seamen across the various important imaginary lines that divide up the globe: the International Date Line, the Arctic and Antarctic circles, and, most especially, the Equator.

Before the war, those on passenger vessels (at least those passengers on the upper decks) would celebrate crossing the Equator with revelry, including singing and dancing, sumptuous treats, and the consumption of a great deal of alcohol. A King Neptune would be crowned, and those "crossing the line" for the first time would be required to pay him homage. In the prewar civilian world, it was all in good fun!

The maritime services had their own way of celebrating the crossing, and, even in peacetime, the initiation took a more sinister turn. It was more like a hazing, than a celebration. Aboard *Orca*, the crew was divided along the lines of the Shellbacks, those who had already been initiated into the rites of King Neptune (those who had already crossed the Equator), and the Pollywogs (those who had not). Unlike other navies, the United States Navy has long been a prohibition navy, and consumption of alcoholic beverages aboard ship is strictly prohibited. That does put a bit of a crimp in crossing-the-line ceremonies. But the American sailor is, if nothing else, innovative, and inevitably finds a way to celebrate important events at sea despite such obstacles.

All of the officers, with the single exception of Ensign Salton, and all of the chiefs, except Chief Francis O'Grady, were shellbacks, as were most of the other senior petty officers, and some of the older seamen. It was their job to ensure that the pollywogs were subjected to as many indignities as possible prior to the actual crossing, when they would be initiated into the sacred rites. The indignities invariably involved in the said initiation included salt water, some nudity, hot sauce, something nasty to drink, a bilge water bath, or perhaps a seawater shower, and, invariably, axle grease.

Lawlor, as ship's captain, and a shellback from his destroyer days, served merely as an observer to the festivities, and not as a participant. His job was to remain entirely neutral during the ceremonies. It was up to the executive officer, Lieutenant Himmelfarb, to make sure the ceremonies did not get out of hand, or result in anyone suffering major harm.

Chief Boatswain Mate Bucky Buckner, the Chief of the Boat, of course, was not only the overall master of ceremonies, but was also the chief tormentor. It was Bucky who personally set forth the order of the initiation ceremony, and it was Bucky who mixed up the official cocktail, concocted of some lube oil, seawater, raw eggs, vinegar, cigarette butts, and a giant bottle of Tabasco sauce. The ceremony itself was presided over by the Royal Baby, he who held court in the name of King Neptune, and it was he to whom every pollywog owed unabashed obeisance. *Orca's* Royal Baby that day was Torpedoman Chief Walakurski, who was the shellback with the largest girth.

Probably for the first time in their careers, those who were pollywogs looked forward to standing watch, and, temporarily at least, escaping the harassment going on below. The pollywogs were first required to assemble in the forward torpedo room wearing nothing but their undershorts. There were some twenty-three of them: one officer and twenty-two enlisted, including Chief O'Grady.

There, in the torpedo room, Bucky berated them as to what lowly creatures they were, how thoroughly unworthy they were to participate in these sacred initiation rites, and how they must be purified before being allowed to "cross the sacred line." The first purification rite involved splashing buckets of bilgewater, followed by buckets of seawater, over the entire lowly assembly.

Ensign Salton and Chief O'Grady were, as the most senior 'wogs, especially targeted, but joined in the spirit of the celebration with as much good grace as they could muster. Of course, given a generous mug of Bucky's cocktail to drink, they only got a swallow or two down, before it came directly back up again, much to the amusement of the shellbacks. Each and every 'wog was required to drink in turn, and only a handful were able to hold the mixture down—only to suffer later for their display of such fortitude.

The culmination of the festivities was the final initiation ceremony, where, still in the forward torpedo room, the pollywogs were required to kiss the belly of the Royal Baby. Chief Walakurski—the Royal Baby—was perched forward, in front of the torpedo tubes, seated on a makeshift throne made from a packing crate and some old blankets. He wore only an oversized diaper and a crown fashioned from a #10 tin can by one of the machinist mates. He wielded a scepter fashioned from a broom handle, and held an orange for an orb; his belly had been smeared with a mixture of axle grease and hair clippings. The pollywogs, still wearing only their skivvies, were again doused with seawater, and were subjected to jibes and insults from the assembled shellbacks as they crawled forward on all fours. Once they had crawled the length of the torpedo room, and had arrived at his throne, they had to there kiss the belly of the Royal Baby.

Having kissed the belly of the Royal Baby, they immediately became shellbacks. A few then joined in with the harassing of the remaining pollywogs. The festivities were, of course, timed so that none of the pollywogs just coming off watch missed out on their initiations.

Once it was over, and all the initiates, and the Royal Baby himself, had gotten cleaned up (insofar as that is possible at sea in a submarine; cleanup usually requiring a saltwater shower and special soap), they were awarded certificates ginned up by Yeoman Bates, proclaiming that each and every one of them were now Shellbacks, members of the Ancient and Mystic Order of the Deep, and having officially served in King Neptune's Court.

These certificates were precious — proof that should the bearers ever "cross the line" again, that they were already King Neptune's loyal subjects.

The Crucifixion

The crowd in the courtroom waited in silent anticipation. The judge was about to pronounce sentence on the convicted felon, Joshua Crowley.

"Mr. Crowley," the judge began, "you stand before this court having plead guilty to a breach of city ordinance 601d. Do you have anything to say before I pronounce sentence on you?"

"Yes, Your Honor. I want to say that I'm really sorry for what I did."

"Be that as it may, Mr. Crowley, you have admitted your guilt, and it is now my duty to pronounce sentence. Mr. Crowley, in light of the seriousness of your crime, I am sentencing you to two hours of crucifixion."

There was a corporate gasp from all the onlookers in the courtroom. Ignoring that, the judge concluded: "This punishment is to be carried out immediately."

As Crowley was being led off to the punishment site, outside the courthouse, the reporters crowded around the judge, who was accompanied by the court bailiff. One said, "Judge, you have pronounced a really unusual punishment on Joshua Crowley. Crucifixion? Really?"

"Certainly, sir," the judge responded testily, "and why not? The Romans used it most effectively, after all, to chastise the unruly for several centuries, did they not? I personally don't think we should turn our noses up over what was so obviously an effective method for maintaining the peace."

A second reporter said, "But Your Honor, the Romans used it as a method of execution!"

"I know that!" the judge shot back. "But to execute people, the Romans had to let them hang on the cross for days. In some cases, up to three full days of crucifixion were required before a criminal expired. This miscreant must endure a mere two hours. Sufficient punishment, I should think, for the heinous crime of . . . " He turned to the bailiff standing beside him and whispered, "What was it the man was convicted of?"

"Jaywalking, Your Honor," the bailiff replied.

". . . jaywalking," the judge finished saying.

"I see, Your Honor," the reporter said, and the others around him nodded their heads in solemn understanding.

As the judge's press conference was breaking up, Joshua Crowley, handcuffed between two policemen, arrived at the field of punishment. It was a beautiful day: the sun was shining; it was warm and calm; and the sky was cloudless. A crowd of spectators had already begun to assemble, as Crowley was told to sit on a lawn chair to await his punishment. A flatbed truck soon arrived at the scene and threaded its way through the crowd. A large wooden cross was lying in the bed of the truck. Four men left the truck cab and pulled the cross out of the truck bed and set it on the ground in front of Crowley. It was placed so that the foot of the cross was over a deep post hole that had already been dug. One of them went back to the truck cab and returned with a large canvas bag.

"Stand up, Crowley," one of the policemen ordered, and Crowley complied. "Strip," he continued. "Everything off but your undershorts—including your shoes and socks." Again, Crowley complied. Soon he stood before the crowd, in nothing but his undershorts. His skinny white body stood in contrast to the gaily colored boxers he wore, and some in the crowd snickered. Despite the warm sunshine, Crowley had goosebumps.

The other policeman opened an envelope and read its contents aloud for the benefit of the assembled crowd. "Joshua Crowley, you have been duly convicted of violation of city ordinance 601d, in that you were arrested, in this city, for crossing Northern Boulevard in the middle of the street, and between two intersections. We are now carrying out the sentence of the court."

He then addressed Crowley. "Lay down on the cross, Crowley, and spread your arms out." Crowley complied. The four men from the truck then set about their business. One proceeded to mount a wooden footrest, a triangular block which resembled a tire chock, and nailed it in place so that Crowley's feet would rest on it with his knees slightly bent when the cross was erected.

As the footrest was being set, another of the men removed three spikes from the canvas bag. Taking one of the two short ones, and using a large maul, he unceremoniously nailed Crowley's left wrist to the crosspiece. Crowley let out a blood-curdling scream as the nail hit home. Some in the observing crowd snickered, but most were horrified. But none turned away as the second nail was driven through Crowley's right wrist. Crowley had passed out by the time the

35

longest spike was driven through his two overlapped feet and into the footrest. But he was awake when the foot of the cross was aligned with the post hole and the cross raised into the vertical position. One of the policemen started a stopwatch. It was just a few minutes past noon.

Hanging on the cross, Crowley's body's weight was supported alternatively by either his outstretched arms, or by his legs pushing up against a footrest. As either his arms or legs tired, he shifted from one system of support to the other. Each shift involved excruciating pain. With his weight supported by his arms, his lungs filled with fluid, and it became more and more difficult for him to breathe. Crowley therefore increasingly used his legs for support, and to avoid asphyxiation.

As the judge had correctly stated, in Roman times, victims could hang on a cross for days before eventually dying. Nonetheless, in the course of his hours on the cross, Crowley experienced both blood loss from the wounds in his wrists and feet, and excruciating pain as he struggled to breathe.

As the day wore on, the crowd tired of the spectacle, and began to disband. When the two hours had passed, one of the policemen was still there, as was the flatbed and its four occupants. When the policeman stopped his stopwatch, he nodded to the others, and then called for an ambulance on his cell phone. One of the four proceeded to mount a ladder and cut off the heads of the nails through Crowley's hands and feet. Crowley whimpered as another of the men, on second ladder, supported him around the waist, while the first one lifted his wrists off the spikes. Then, together, they lifted his body up so that his feet cleared the long spike that held them to the footrest. Then they laid Crowley flat on the ground to await the ambulance. As Crowley still lay there, the four men lifted the cross from the post hole, loaded it on the truck, and drove away.

The ambulance arrived as the truck was leaving. The EMTs loaded Crowley on a stretcher, and attended to him in transit to the city hospital. His sentence carried out, hands and feet bandaged, Crowley was released the next day under his own recognizance. As he left the hospital, just two reporters were there to interview him.

"What was it like . . . being crucified?" the one asked.

"Painful," Crowley replied. "It was so bad I was really afraid I was going to die. I knew in my head I probably wouldn't, but that didn't matter in the least while I hung there. Nobody should have to go through what I went through."

"So," the other reporter asked, "are you angry with the judge for having you crucified?"

"Oh no," Crowley replied. "The judge was absolutely right. I will never, ever, jaywalk again."

The Tide of War

The old man had no idea why the enemy had been shelling throughout the day, the artillery flashes off in the distance. His own country's artillery had been firing from the west, and now the enemy from the east — shells always flying overhead in both directions. Nonetheless, both sides had remained more or less where they had been for the past few weeks. What he *did* know was that the shells landing and exploding in his pasture were tearing up nothing more than soil these days; the shells having long since destroyed the grass that once nourished his sheep.

But that was of no consequence; his own country's army had come and taken all his sheep when the war first started. "Our soldiers must eat, if they are to fight for your freedom," he was told by the grim lieutenant who gave him a voucher — to be redeemed at the end of the conflict — for his forty-two sheep.

Thus far, the enemy shells had missed the hovel he called his home. He thought that perhaps God had need of a witness to the destruction being rained on his country by the enemy. It would be so much easier for him if one of the shells had blown the place up while he slept inside it. Instead, it remained intact; even the flower garden and the patch of grass in front remained untouched.

What he did thank God for was that he had taken his wife long since, and that she had not been forced to witness any of this. They had not had much, not since they were first married, years and years ago, but they had had enough, and it was a good life. They had the pasture for the sheep, the milk cow, and the two horses; they had the vegetable garden in back, alongside the pens for the pigs and chickens. A spring-fed brook running at the edge of the forest had supplied plenty of water for drinking, cooking, and cleaning.

But the shells had torn up the vegetable garden just as they had the pasture, and, before coming for the sheep, the army had come for the horses, the pigs, and chickens (ah, but he had been given vouchers for them!). Then the milk cow had dried up for lack of freshening. Reluctantly, he had slaughtered her himself, salting and drying her flesh, giving him something for sustenance beyond what greens and tubers he could gather in the forest. Soon, the last of her meat would be gone, too, just as most of the forest was also gone: trees and underbrush torn asunder by the relentless shelling. Even the mice had left the place. Only the brook remained, its course altered somewhat, but still providing fresh water.

That night, even asleep, his mind had registered the change. The explosions going off all around him now were fewer and far between. There was also a new sound. The faint sound of "friendly" artillery off in the west was now louder, the whistling of the shells as they passed overhead somehow different. *Ah!* the old man thought, *the counter-offensive! The enemy is finally in retreat!*

At dawn, as the old man arose (out of habit, now, since the animals he had tended all his life were now nonexistent), he could hear the sound of his own country's armor advancing, tank treads screeching down the rough roadway as they approached.

By noon, he saw them, the battle tanks, advancing down the road at a snail's pace, moving east, each of the belching behemoths with its trail of soldiers tagging behind in ordered disarray. The noise was loud, different, but far more preferable to the old man than that of the exploding enemy shells. And, as the tanks advanced, the shells whistling overhead, relentlessly flying toward the enemy, increased apace. And the flashes of light from the west and from the east were different, and in a good way. The counterattack had begun in earnest, and the enemy was in retreat.

Not that, for the old man at least, the situation was really any different. His ravaged land was being ravaged all the more. The edge of his pasture was now a stinking latrine, serving the troops of his own nation encamped there and in the ravaged meadow beyond.

But the tanks, at least, continued to roll east, taking the fight to the enemy.

The captain came from the camp, astride his great horse, and said, "There is really nothing here for you any more, *pochtennyy*. It might be better for you to travel north. There are refugee camps there away from this constant shelling."

"There is nowhere safe," the old man replied, "and there is nothing for me in the north. This land, despoiled as it is, is *my* land, my father's land, and his father's land before him. All that I am, or ever will be, is here. No, there is nothing for me in the north."

The captain shook his head, stirred his horse (who had been grazing on the patch of grass still undisturbed in front of the old man's hovel), and returned to the camp.

Fast planes flew by that same day, and, later, helicopters, the enemy craft sending rockets into the camp, destroying all that was there, killing, destroying. *Nothing could survive such destruction,* the old man observed. *Everything and everyone alive there are gone forever.*

But, once again, the old man's hovel stood untouched. There was death around him everywhere, but somehow it had not yet taken him. Perhaps he would survive this war after all.

The next morning the old man awoke to find the captain's horse, which had somehow survived the holocaust at the camp, grazing on the small patch of grass in front of his place. *God,* the old man then knew, *God is still alive.*

He had expected his country's tanks to come rolling back, in full retreat before the enemy. But they did not. Instead, fresh troops from the west came marching down the roadway, young men and women marching behind yet more tanks. All were headed east, and the flashes of light from the enemy artillery were dimming all the more. *Perhaps the counter-offensive has worked, and the enemy is being pushed back,* the old man prayed.

One of the passing soldiers stopped off and took the captain's horse. "Army property," the soldier said. "See the brand," he pointed. Evidence. Perhaps it was just as well. Horses were good company, but the old man really had nothing for the beast to eat. The patch of grass in front of his hut, after all, would have been chewed bare in no time at all. The old man sighed as the animal was led away. It was just as well indeed; in desperation he might have slaughtered the horse just for something to eat.

Now the whistling sound of the shells passing overhead from the east had stopped. He had seen his country's artillery towed behind trucks and heading east, looking to set up and fire from fresh positions. For one day only, they had set up in the pasture, and were firing from there. The din had been almost unbearable. Thankfully, they moved further down the road the next day, and, eventually, as the counter offensive rolled east, the noise went with it.

But soon there *was* nothing to eat. The milk cow's meat was gone, and the edible greens and roots in the forest had long since been picked clean. He had set traps in hope of catching some small animal, and had used the last of the salted beef to bait them, but they had come up empty. Now, even the bait was gone. The brook still ran — he would at least not die of thirst — but that would only prolong the inevitable. *How long can one live without food?* he wondered, fearful that he would soon find out. *God, are you still there? Are you still alive?*

Two days passed, and he had not eaten. The old man lay on his bed for no other reason than to conserve his energy. In sleep, he had dreams of his wife, saw her welcoming him into the realm of the dead. In his dream, he had been more than willing to join her. But whenever he was awake, he clung to life.

Another day passed, and the old man grew weary of just lying there, starving. He thought of the captain's horse, wondering to himself what he might have done if the horse had not been taken away by that soldier. Would he have slaughtered and eaten it? Or would he have mounted it, and ridden north to the refugee camps, as the captain had urged? *No, I am an old man, and set in my ways. I would have slaughtered the beast and eaten it, and I would not be starving now! Still, there is nothing for me here now but starvation and death. Perhaps I should at least try walking north. It would be something to do, rather than just lie here.*

The old man got up from his bed and went out of the hut. It was early morning; the sun was still quite low in the east. On the edge of the pasture a small, temporary camp of sorts had been set up: a large lorry, a small tent, and three soldiers. They had lit a campfire, and were preparing breakfast. *Food!* the old man thought, and approached the camp.

"I'm hungry," the old man announced to the seated troops, one woman and two men. "I haven't eaten in three days."

"We can't have that, now, can we, *pochtennyy*," one of the men said. "Come. Sit. Join us."

The old man was happy to accept the invitation and a tin plate of beans and cabbage. "Slowly," the woman said, as he began to wolf down the food. "Eat it slowly, or you will just puke it back up." He knew she was right, and forced himself to slow down.

He learned that they were a rear guard on the way to the front, their truck loaded with food to feed the troops in their battalion. "We must be on our way. We can't stay in one place too long. The enemy drones are everywhere. But we cannot leave you here like this. You really belong in one of the displaced persons camps to the north."

"I don't want to leave here. This is my home," he explained.

"But you must," she said. "There is nothing for you here. You will starve here, no?"

"Perhaps," the old man admitted. "But at least I will die in my home, and on my land."

The woman sighed, and going to the truck, extracted a sack of potatoes, and some cabbages from the back. "Here," she said, "take these and go north." One of the men started to object to her giving away food meant for the troops, but one look from the woman silenced him.

The old man watched as the three broke camp and started east in the truck, the sack of potatoes and the cabbages at his feet. He figured that if he was careful, he could make the potatoes and the cabbages last for weeks. *God,* the old man knew, *God is still alive.*

THE LORRY, EMPTY NOW, MADE its way east to get another load. As they passed by the old man's hut, the woman insisted they stop. As the three approached the hut, there was no mistaking the odor of death about the place. Inside the hut, they found the old man on his bed, dead. "Looks like he just stopped breathing," the woman said. "He was old, and God took him. At least he didn't die of starvation. We must bury him." Again, when one of the others started to object, the woman silenced him with a look.

They buried the old man out behind the hut. When the soldiers left, they were careful to retrieve what was left of the potatoes and cabbages and take them away with them. Waste not, want not. After all, there was a war on.

The Shadow People

I know you've seen them, too. The creatures that flit back behind you, the ones you catch just out of the corner of your eye, when you turn around quickly. I've developed the habit of looking for them—catching them—just before they flit into my shadow. Always hiding there, just out of sight, I call them the shadow people. I've watched for them, glimpsed them just behind other people, if only for an instant or so. I know for sure I'm not the only one they follow.

I told my wife, Margo, about them, and she just laughed and said I was seeing things. That's when I figured that marrying Margo, a long time back, had not been such a good idea after all. Although I must admit it did *seem* so at the time.

But I digress, and I know what you're thinking: If the shadow people follow other people, and I can see them, why can't those others? That's a stupid question, really. They simply aren't looking for them, as I am. Think about it. Say you're looking at another person. Well, they are solid. You can't see through them now, can you? They block your view. That's why you can't see who's lurking behind them, in their shadow!

Not that the shadow people have any real substance. Flesh and blood couldn't possibly move that fast. They're more than likely made of effluvium, or some such stuff. Stuff you can see, but couldn't hold onto, no matter how quick you were, or how hard you tried. I know. I've reached out — ever so quickly — to catch one behind me, at least a million times. And I always close my fingers around nothing. Nothing whatever. Like I said, effluvium, or some such.

"What the hell's wrong with you, Mark?" Margo would say. "You're always jiggin' and twitchin,' jerkin' around like someone's followin' you, and you wanna catch 'em unawares."

I try to explain it to her, but she just laughs some more, and says I'm seeing things again. Always so sure of herself, so self-righteous. Made me want to murder her.

I'd have done it much sooner, if it hadn't been for my old truck, name of Sweet Thing, keeping me sane. She was such a Sweet Thing! Old '55 Ford F150, light green, stepside pickup in mint condition — all original parts. And she runs like a top, even if I had to tune her back, so she'd run on today's shitty unleaded gasoline. Even the shadow people admired her, I know they did, and I'd try to catch them looking as I worked on her — polishing and shining her, and tuning her up. "Sometimes, I think you love that ol' truck more'n you love me," Margo would say — and she was right.

It came to a head just the other day. We were out repairing a bit of fence, Margo and I, and I was pounding in a staple with a hammer, while Margo held the fencing in place, and I just caught one of them out of the corner of my eye . . .

"Quit yer jerkin' dammit!" she shouted at me.

I got angry with her, and her always doubting me, and . . . I guess . . . I flew off the handle just a bit — and I hit her. Hard. With the hammer. First time ever I hit her, I think, and I didn't mean to hurt her. Not really. But I did.

"Margo," I said, "you all right? I'm sorry, Babe, I didn't mean to hit you so hard, I just flew off the handle. Speak to me, Baby, you okay?"

But she wasn't okay. She was dead.

And that was when the shadow people started talking to me. "Now look at what you've gone and done," one of them, said, behind me.

I sat there a while. Just sat there, at the base of the fencepost. I cried a bit. And I'm sure I could hear one of 'em crying behind me as well. I'm sure of it.

After a while — it had to be just past noon, 'cause the Sun was up high and bright, and it was hot, and I was getting hungry — I figured I needed to do something about Margo's body. There's this spot on the farm — there's this hill there — and, on it is a nice full maple tree that Margo used to like. I figured maybe I should bury her there. So, I got a shovel from the barn, and went to that place and started to dig. The whole time, I knew they was watching me — the shadow people. But no matter how hard I tried, just like always, I could not turn quickly enough to see them. By the time I had dug a hole big enough, and deep enough, it was well past dinner time and I was really, really hungry.

So, I went to the house and had some of the ham out of the fridge Margo had cooked the day before, and some of the bread she had baked that morning, and made

49

myself a sandwich. After I washed it all down with a glass of milk, I felt somewhat better. I washed my plate and my glass and set them on the rack to dry, just like Margo always says to do, and put the ham back in the fridge. Waste not, want not.

I know they were still watching me when I went to the barn to get the wheelbarrow so I could move Margo's body.

After I buried her, along with the hammer, I said a few words: some bits of prayers I could remember, you know, and some nice things about Margo. It was starting to get dark by then, so I put the wheelbarrow back in the barn, and went up into the house. They watched me as I ate some more ham, watched some TV—I really like to watch TV. Margo always says I watch way too much TV—and then went to bed.

A COUPLE OF WEEKS PASSED, and nobody seemed to notice Margo was missing. Then, her sister in Hartford called, and I told her Margo couldn't come to the phone 'cause she was out shopping.

"But it's Sunday," she said. "My sister is a good Christian woman, and she would never go shopping on Sunday."

"Well today, she did," I said, and hung up on her.

She called again a couple of times after that, and each time I made some excuse or 'tother as to why Margo couldn't come to the phone, but I know none of them satisfied her.

"She's getting suspicious," a shadow person behind me said.

"I know," I answered, "but there's not much I can do about it." I turned quick so's I could catch a glimpse of him, but he had gone.

The next time her sister called, I told her Margo had packed up and left me

"Bullshit," her sister said. She always had a mouth on her. "She would never go off and do that without telling me. I don't believe you."

"Well, it's the truth," I said. "She's gone, and never comin' back." That time, her sister hung up on me.

"You told her she left you," a lady shadow person said. "Now someone's bound to come lookin' for her. Best you get rid of her things."

"Good idea," I said, and turned quick again to see if I could see her, but that shadow person was as quick as all the others—way quicker'n me. I packed up all Margo's geegaws and buried them back of the barn. Her clothes, I burned.

A couple of days later, the sheriff came around. He was a heavyset guy, in full county mounty uniform, green top and brown pants, about my height.

"Some lady from Hartford called, sayin' your wife's gone missing, Mr. Fellows. Says she's . . . Margo's . . . sister."

"Don't know how missing she is," I said, "but she sure as blazes ain't here. Packed up and left me weeks ago." I could hear the shadow people snickering behind me, and hoped the sheriff couldn't hear 'em.

"Okay," the sheriff said, "but if you don't mind, Mr. Fellows, is it okay if I look around your property, and, maybe in the house?"

"You got a warrant?" I asked. I knew my rights.

"No, sir, I don't," he allowed, "but I'm sure I could get one." He squinted up his face a bit. "You got something to hide?"

"Nope," I said. "But I don't like people snoopin' 'round for no reason, neither."

"You tell him, that fat bastard," a voice behind me said.

"Okay, Mr. Fellows, if that's the way you want to play it. Have a nice day, sir. I'll be back," he said, turned and left.

"Shit," a voice behind me said.

"Shit," I agreed.

I've seen how these policemen operate on TV. I knew it was just a matter of time before they would come back around and catch me. I had to have forgotten something — some trinket or other in our room. Maybe I left some sign back up on the hill where she was buried — disturbed soil, maybe, like you always see on TV — and maybe some more where I had buried her stuff. They were sure to catch me. On TV, they *always* catch the bad guy.

"You're screwed," a voice behind me said. "You better run."

"Where the hell am I gonna run?" I answered. "Besides, even if you run, they still catch you anyway. Always do on TV."

"True that," another voice answered. "So what you gonna do now?"

I knew exactly what I had to do now. I went out to the barn and got into my truck — Sweet Thing that it was! I drove out to the reservoir off route 320. Margo and I would sometimes go out there and picnic when we were first married, but not too much since then. Brother and I, we used to swim there as kids. I could swim it all the way across back then, and I bet I could do it again — if I had to.

I knew the shadow people had climbed into the back of the pickup. No way the bastards were going to let me go off anywhere on my own. But what they didn't know is that I had a plan now — a plan to lose them.

When we got to the reservoir, I parked and locked Sweet Thing in the parking lot and walked down to the reservoir. Didn't want nobody stealing her. The beach was empty. Not surprising, this time of the year — early yet. Water's way too cold for regular folks. I stripped naked and got into the water. Slowly. Damn, but it was cold! No matter. I knew the shadow people would follow me in anyway.

I began to swim out, and was maybe about fifty, sixty feet out when I did a quick flip to see if I could catch them, but even in the water they were fast! No matter. My plan was I would go out far enough, maybe even all the way to the other side, like I could do when I was a kid. They'd be sure to chicken out and turn back, and that way I'd be sure to lose them — for good! So, I just kept swimming, I figured, heading for the other side. Bye, bye, shadow people! Damn, but that water was cold.

Gene Masters

Ghost Boat

To the captain and her crew, the boat was a living, breathing, being—a being animated by the collection of individuals that served aboard her. The captain understood this, just as he understood that his mission was to be her main life force, tasked to guide her by guiding the men under his command, the men who also served her.

It was very early morning, the sun was still just below the horizon, and the boat was about to make a dangerous daylight surface. The captain, waiting in the conning tower while the diving officer brought the boat slowly up to periscope depth, wanted to be the first one up on the bridge, just in case.

"At five-eight feet, Captain," the diving office sung out from down below in the control room.

"Five-eight feet, aye," the captain acknowledged, and then said, "Up periscope." He rode the scope up as it cut through the surface, and made a deliberate 360-degree sweep.

Only minutes before, sonar had also done an all-around sweep, and had heard nothing, reporting "No contacts." No matter. Nothing was as sure as the old Mark-1 eyeball, and, indeed there were no contacts in sight.

"Down scope," the captain ordered, then added, "Surface the boat."

Immediately, the *"Oh-ou-gah! Oh-ou-gah! Oh-ou-gah!"* triple cry of the claxon sounded throughout the boat, followed by the spoken words, "Surface, surface, surface," broadcast over the 1-MC. Below, in the control room, the Chief-of-the-Watch opened the valves on the hydraulic manifold that filled the ballast tanks with compressed air, forcing out the water they held, giving the boat positive buoyancy. Standing on the ladder that led from the conning tower to the bridge, the captain cracked open the bridge hatch as the boat broached the surface, oblivious to the seawater that spilled down over his shoulders. When the shower stopped, he popped open the hatch, and climbed his way quickly topside. When he stood upright on her bridge, for just an instant, he admired the beauty that was his command: this lethal lady beneath his feet, who, properly animated, dealt out death and destruction to the enemy. The boat. His war bride. And, if he treated her right, they would all again survive this day.

"Lookouts, up!" he shouted down to the conning tower, and within moments, four lookouts had taken their place in the shears, all five men on deck now scanning the horizon through their binoculars. Simultaneously, the boat's four diesels sprang, rumbling, to life, as the enginemen below lit them off, and the maneuvering watch, in the next compartment aft, switched the boat's electric motors from battery to diesel propulsion.

Normally, the captain would have ordered the low-pressure blowers started up, finishing the blow, and raising the boat fully to the surface. But not this day; these were enemy waters, after all, so the captain left her decks awash. He could well afford to do so: the sea was a smooth blue mirror, lit only by the shimmering shaft of light cast from the coming Sun. The only disturbance in that mirror was the boat's wake, smooth ripples off the bow and stern as she cut through the water, and, just aft, the bubbly foam made by the diesel fumes exhausting below the waterline.

The sea air was moist, hot, oppressive. As the captain scanned the horizon, he mused that this, his fifth war patrol aboard the boat, his fourth as its commander, had been its most fruitless. It was now three years into the war, and enemy targets were becoming scarce. There was no way he would risk his boat in a daylight surface in these waters just a year ago.

"Permission to come up!" the executive officer called up from the conning tower.

"Come up," the captain replied, and then the XO was standing alongside him.

"There's an intermittent blip on the air search radar, Skipper, off to the southwest. Doesn't appear to be coming our way."

"Better keep an eye on him. We're sitting ducks up here."

"Roger that. Will do, Skipper." He paused, then change the subject. "Engineer says the diesels have sucked 3A and 3B fuel oil ballast tanks dry. Want permission to switch them over to ballast tanks."

The captain thought about that. *Could use two extra ballast tanks – get the boat up and own quicker. First couple of dives would be messy though. Until the tanks wash clean out,*

57

any residual fuel would leave an oil slick. Great marker for any destroyer looking to blow the old girl out of the water. Still, getting up and down quicker would help her if the attacker was airborne . . .

"Yeah, okay. Tell him to go ahead. Let me know when the switch is made, and then make sure all the watch standers know they have two more ballast tanks to open and shut on the hydraulic manifold."

"It'll be obvious. The padlocks on the valve handles will be gone."

"Nonetheless . . ."

"Aye, Skipper, will do. Should I set the regular watch?"

"Yeah, go ahead. But I think I'll still stay up here for a while."

"Yessir. Permission to go below."

"Granted." And the XO left the bridge.

Forty-five minutes later, the regular watch set, the word came up to the officer of the deck, and to the captain, who was still on the bridge, that external tanks 3A and 3B were now rigged as ballast tanks, and that the word had been passed to all watch standers.

"Very well," the OOD acknowledged, and started to formally report to the captain. "Sir, the Engineer Officer reports—"

"Got it," the captain said. "Tanks 3 A and B are now ballast tanks."

"Yessir," the OOD acknowledged.

The captain had finally decided to leave the bridge, when the aft port lookout shouted, "Contact! Plane, way out, coming at us out of the sun!"

"Clear the bridge!" the OOD shouted instinctively, as he pushed over the lever that sounded the claxon, twice, and shouted "Dive! Dive!" into the 1-MC. By then the captain had already scrambled down the hatch and was in the conning tower.

The boat was already on its way down, its propulsion switched from the diesels to the battery, when the OOD followed the four lookouts scrambling down through the bridge hatch. Seconds later, the OOD was below in the control room, and had taken charge of the dive. "Green board, Sir!" he shouted up to the conning tower, confirming that the indicator board lights, those that showed the position of the boat's ballast tank valves, were all green. The valves were open, and the ballast tanks were flooding; the lady they served was responding as she was designed to do.

"Very well," the captain acknowledged from the conning tower. "Make your depth one-zero-zero feet, and smartly!"

"One-zero-zero feet, smartly, Sir!" the OOD-turned-diving-officer responded. Then, to the plane operators he said, "Full dive on the bow and stern planes. Twenty degrees down bubble, one-zero-zero feet!"

The men operating the bow and stern planes acknowledged the order, and the boat was well on its way down. The boat was doing just as she was being urged to do, passing through sixty feet, when the diving officer ordered, "Blow negative to the mark," and the chief of the watch at the hydraulic manifold opened the compressed air valve to negative tank, blowing out just enough of the water in the tank to restore the boat to neutral diving trim, and slow the dive. The bubble was ordered eased off in increments, until, not yet five minutes into the dive, just like the obedient lady she was, the boat settled out at one hundred feet.

"Watch your depth!" the captain shouted down from the conning tower. "I'm going to slow 'er down."

"Aye, Captain."

Then the captain ordered, "All ahead slow. Make turns for three knots."

The order was acknowledged, and then passed on to the maneuvering room. Then: "Pass the word quietly: general quarters, all hands man your battle stations."

In another four minutes, all hands were at their battle stations. The XO had joined the captain in the conning tower; the engineer officer had the dive; the chief of the boat was at the hydraulic manifold; and all stations were manned by their most-qualified submariner.

"Sonar, contacts?" the captain asked.

"No contacts," the sonar operator reported.

"Very well. Keep your ears open. I'm gonna bring her up to periscope depth." Then, to the diving officer, "Bring her up slowly. Make your depth five-eight feet."

"Five-eight feet, slowly, aye. Five-degree up bubble."

When the boat was passing sixty feet, the captain ordered, "Up scope," and, as the search periscope rose from its well, he rode it up. The lens had just broken the surface and the captain began a 360-degree sweep of the horizon. He was about halfway around when he said,

"Holy crap! There's a damn carrier up here! Bearing, mark!"

"Bearing two-seven-seven," the quartermaster read from the scope's bezel.

The captain guessed the carrier's mast height at forty feet, and set the stadimeter. He adjusted the scope optics so that an image of the carrier was brought down until its topmost mast was at the waterline. "Range!"

"Four thousand, two hundred."

The captain completed the sweep, settling the scope back on the carrier. "No other contacts. Down scope." Then, "Sonar? You didn't hear that bastard?"

"No Sir!" The sonarman was adamant. "Not a whisper, Sir!"

"What you see, Captain?" the XO asked.

"Carrier. An old one — one of their original cruiser conversions — conning tower on the left. See for yourself," he said, and relinquished the scope to the XO.

"Thought all of those were either sunk or retired," the XO said, turning the scope back over to the captain.

"Not this one, apparently. Still, it did look like it'd seen better days!"

"What about that plane?" the XO asked.

"Never got a chance to angle up the scope optics and search for it. Tell you what — you man the search scope, and look for it, while I go on the attack scope and check out that carrier again. Still haven't figured out why sonar can't hear him — unless maybe he's dead in the water."

Seven minutes after the first sighting, both scopes were raised; there was no sign of the aircraft, and the carrier was indeed dead in the water.

"Firing solution?" the captain asked the torpedo data computer operator.

"Yessir, Captain," the TDC operator replied. "Based on the two observations, the target's not moving. Recommend we come about to last bearing. Then it'll be pretty much a straight shot."

"Very well. Come left to two-seven-three."

"Left to two-seven-three," the sailor manning the helm acknowledged.

The captain ordered three torpedo tubes forward made ready, and told the TDC operator he planned to fire a spread of three fish at the carrier, and to set the second and third shots one-half degree, first left, and then right, of the base torpedo course.

When the boat was settled out on course 273, the captain ordered the attack scope up, did a sweep of the horizon and found no other contacts, then said, "Final bearing, mark!"

"Two-seven-four."

"Final range, mark!"

"Eighteen hundred fifty yards."

The TDC operator dialed in the updated numbers.

Seconds later, the first of three Mark-14 steam-powered torpedoes was on its way to the target, followed by two others, each a second apart.

"Fast screws approaching, bearing zero-seven-one!" the sonar operator sung out.

"What in hell?" the XO exclaimed. "There was nothing there! I swear there was nothing there!"

Swinging the scope around to the indicated bearing, the captain said, "There is now—destroyer, bow on, about six thousand yards out! Take her down, fast! Two-hundred feet — right full rudder — all ahead flank!"

"Two hundred feet," the diving officer acknowledged. "Flood negative! Full dive on the bow and stern planes! Twenty-five degrees down bubble!"

The boat was well on its way down when three explosions were heard in succession off to port. All three torpedoes had hit their mark, and the living lady they served had left her lethal mark upon the enemy. But there was to be no celebration, not with a destroyer bearing down on them. "Rig for depth charge!" The order was passed throughout the boat, and water-tight doors and ventilation flappers between the boat's compartments were shut tight.

The first of the depth charges exploded somewhere aft, as the boat passed through one-hundred-fifty feet. It was too far away to do any real damage, but it set up enough concussive force in the water behind the boat that there was a palpable surge, accelerating the boat forward, and straight through the two-hundred-foot mark. The diving officer didn't regain control of the dive until the boat was at two-hundred-twenty feet, and reported the fact to the captain.

"Very well," the captain acknowledged. "Make your depth two-two-zero feet." He ordered the boat slowed to minimum turns, bare steerageway, and settled on a course almost due northwest. "Rig for silent running," he ordered

Off in the distance, waterborne sounds of a ship breaking up could be heard, their target sinking. Several other depth charges went off — all wide of the mark and now only loud noises in the water. Then came the pinging: the destroyer, slow screws now, searching, searching. The diving officer was having trouble maintaining depth; the boat was heavy, and slipping through two-hundred-thirty feet. The lady was being coaxed, but she was not responding. He reported it to the captain, who told him he could have no more speed to help him level off the boat, and to just do the best he could. He ordered that negative tank be blown almost dry, but the boat continued to go deeper, just descending more slowly. The diving officer was final able to hold her at the two-hundred-thirty-foot depth by putting a bubble of compressed air into the bow buoyancy tank, and another in safety tank.

The captain was almost sure that the boat was safe, that she had apparently alluded her hunter, when the pinging suddenly grew louder. Soon, the destroyer was right on top of them, but the enemy had not quite found them; the pinging interval was still long, their sonar still in search mode. The captain changed course ninety degrees left, and added turns to make three knots. The diving officer was grateful for the added speed, and was even able to bring the boat back up some.

We were almost well and gone, my lady, the captain thought. *How in blazes did he ever find us?* Then he thought, *The damn fuel ballast tanks! The sea up there like glass, and we must be trailing just enough of an oil sheen to mark our position! My fault! I've let you down, old girl! Still, the tank vents are shut now, and whatever oil was going to be released has already been — there won't be any more. If we can only clear the dive area . . .*

Just then, the destroyer above switched to short-interval pinging. They had been spotted!

The first of the depth charges exploded directly above them, driving the boat deeper, causing it to list violently, first to port, then to starboard, before she settled out, shattering gage glasses, and causing valves and hull fittings to spring leaks. Worse yet was the terror a near miss spread among the crew as men were thrown to the deck and onto machinery and bulkheads. The boat was blown down through two-hundred-ninety feet, and was still sinking. The lady they served was groaning audibly, crying out in her distress.

"Damage reports!" the captain shouted. Then, all too quickly, that last blast was followed by still others, ever more violent.

She's a thin-skinned boat—just five-eighth-inch steel between us and the sea, he thought. *Three-hundred-twelve-foot test depth . . .*

Damage reports began coming in, even as the boat was being rocked by blast after blast. A sea valve had been carried away in the forward torpedo room, and the compartment was flooding. The men in the compartment bled compressed air into the compartment, pressurizing it. That didn't stop the leak, but only slowed it. And the lady they served continued on deeper, as if the very deep itself was calling out to her . . .

"We're at three hundred fifteen feet, captain, and still going down. Permission to put a bubble in—"

"Do it!" the captain shouted, and ordered speed increased to five knots, as another blast close aboard pushed the boat yet deeper.

Come to me, my lady. The deep calling out.

The diving officer ordered bubbles put in ballast tanks 2A and B. The pressure hull was groaning audibly; occasional snaps and cracking sounds echoed throughout the boat—the lady now screaming in her death throes.

"Three hundred eighty feet, Sir! We're still going down!" Another almost-direct hit, and the boat rocked and bucked; men were tossed about like corks, and there were ever more leaks.

The boat finally groaned a mighty groan, and split apart at the forward battery. The men there died instantly; the rest died as the boat continued to sink, and each sealed compartment imploded in turn, as the lady gave up her spirit to the deep.

IT WAS VERY EARLY THE following morning, the sun was still just below the horizon, and the boat was about to make a dangerous daylight surface. The captain, waiting in the conning tower while the diving officer brought the boat slowly up to periscope depth, wanted to be the first one up on the bridge, just in case.

As always, the boat, a living, breathing being, animated by the men that served aboard her, was responding to their collective will.

"At five-eight feet, Captain," the diving office sung out from down below in the control room.

"Five-eight feet, aye," the captain acknowledged, and then said, "Up periscope." He rode the scope up as it cut through the surface, and made a deliberate 360-degree sweep.

Only minutes before, sonar had also done an all-around sweep, and had heard nothing, reporting "No contacts." No matter. Nothing was as sure as the old Mark-1 eyeball, and, the captain saw that there were indeed no contacts to be seen.

"Down scope," the captain ordered. Then, "Surface the boat.

The bridge hatch popped; the captain climbed his way quickly topside. When he stood upright on her bridge, for just an instant he admired the beauty that was his command: this lethal lady beneath his feet, who, properly animated, dealt out death and destruction to the enemy. The boat. His war bride. Perhaps this day would be different. Perhaps, this day, she would survive.

Gene Masters

The Queue

Harrison couldn't remember when he discovered the queue, but he had to have been very young—young enough to find the waiting line fascinating, that line that stretched all the way up the side of the mountain, stretching out of sight and into the clouds. People waited in the queue patiently, even though the line moved forward exceedingly slowly, fractions of an inch at a time. Harrison only knew that he had to attach himself to it, take his place at the end of the line.

He stayed there for a while, waiting. Others, just as young as he, showed up and took their place behind him. Nobody spoke. They just waited, inching forward when it was time.

Harrison noted that, every once in a while, somebody broke out of the queue and wandered off. One in particular he noticed: a pretty young girl. Harrison left the queue and followed after her.

"Wait up," he said, and the girl looked back at him, smiled, and slowed her pace. He quickly caught up with her. "I'm Harrison," he said.

"I'm Mary."

They walked on, married, and began raising a family.

HARRISON TOOK A JOB IN a small factory. But one day, he felt the need to rejoin the queue.

"I understand," Mary said.

And Harrison walked off and rejoined the line, taking a place at the very end. It was still very long, still stretching up the mountain side, and into the clouds. The only difference Harrison could see now was that the line, though still moving very slowly, was not as slow as it was that first time.

Harrison stayed in the queue for a while — days, surely, but maybe even weeks. People came and took their places behind him. Again, just as it was his first time waiting, nobody spoke. Occasionally, some of those waiting in front of him quit the line and wandered off, just as Mary had done the day they met.

Waiting in the line eventually became very boring — nothing to do but wait, and shuffle imperceptibly forward. No conversation. No human contact.

"This sucks," Harrison eventually said to himself, and he left the line. He left the line because he could, and because he missed Mary and the children.

"Welcome home, Harrison," Mary said. "I'm so happy you're back." And the children squealed in delight, excited to see their father again. And Harrison felt good.

THEN IT BECAME MARY'S TURN to go back to the queue, to take her place at the end of the line. Harrison was devastated when she left, but he knew she had no choice, and also that he was powerless to stop her. He could only wait, and pray for her return.

Eventually, Mary left the line and did come back home. Harrison and the children greeted her return with genuine joy. And now, Mary too, felt good.

TIME PASSED. THE CHILDREN GREW. One by one, they left home and started their own lives, but, for their youngest at least, only after joining the queue and waiting at the end of the line for a time.

MORE TIME PASSED. HARRISON AND Mary settled into the rhythm of their passing days. Once again, inevitably it seemed, Mary said, "I must return," and Harrison knew, sadly, that Mary would leave him and take her place at the end of the queue. He waited and prayed for her return. But this time, Mary never returned. And now he no longer felt good.

THIS TIME, ONLY A SHORT time passed. Once again, Harrison felt the need to go back to the queue and wait on line for a while. This time the line was much shorter; the end of the line, where he took his place, was now far up the mountain, almost at the point where the line of people disappeared into the clouds. And the people, unspeaking, were now moving forward at a perceptible pace.

Harrison had almost reached the place where he would enter the clouds, when he knew again that he might never again be able to leave the queue and return home — not that he particularly looked forward to returning home. Home had become a sterile place. No Mary. No children. No one there to talk to any more, no more than there were waiting in the queue. But, eventually, return home he did, and he did not feel at all good. Now the people there treated him as though he was a child. They talked to each other, but hardly ever to him. Mostly, they talked over him, as if he wasn't even there.

The time finally came when Harrison knew that he must once again take his place at the end of the waiting line. Somehow, although he now had difficulty walking, he managed the walk to the queue quite easily, and take his place at the end of the line. The end of the line was near the very top of the mountain now, well above the clouds, and the air was wet and hazy. Still, Harrison was able to see quite clearly — much more clearly than he was able to see back home. There were far fewer people in front of him now, and only occasionally did someone join the line behind him. The line was also moving, still moving slowly, but now moving steadily forward.

He was close to reaching the summit now, and Harrison noted that the people at the head of the line simply kept walking forward, those at the very front of the line stepping off, one by one, stepping off the edge of the mountaintop, disappearing into nothingness — an abyss below.

At the summit, standing to one side, was a kindly-looking old man, dressed in a flowing white robe, the top of his head as bald as an egg. He wore a broad smile, framed in a flowing white beard, and he spoke to each person in turn as they stepped off the top of the mountain and into the abyss.

It was now Harrison's turn at the summit.

"What must I do?" Harrison asked the old man with the flowing white beard.

"You must step off the top of the mountain," he answered.

"And what will happen when I do?" Harrison asked.

"Well," the old man replied, "it all depends. You will either fall down like a stone onto the rocks below, or you will take off and fly like an eagle."

"It all depends on what?"

"It depends on many things. But mostly it depends on how you lived your life, and how well you loved."

"I see," said Harrison, and he stepped off the summit, into the abyss . . .

Marking Time

He can't remember exactly when he discovered his unique ability, but, once, when he was staring at his watch, the sweep second hand started moving backwards.

He didn't think anything of it at first, assuming that his watch was somehow defective. But then, it happened again. And then again and again. The longer he stared at it, the longer the second hand moved backwards. Yet, no matter how many times he observed this phenomenon, and the watch had started back forwards, it had never lost time, and was always in general agreement with other accurate timepieces.

He began to see if he could hold his concentration long enough to observe the backward motion for a complete minute. He eventually did, and sure enough, the minute hand had reversed direction as well. He worked at it, and was able to do concentrate long enough to reverse his watch for almost three full minutes.

Then, once, when he was staring at the timepiece, with its second hand moving in reverse, he noted a large black ant crawling on the ground in front of him. It was, like the second hand, also moving backwards. The realization broke his concentration, and, just as the second hand began to move forward again, so did the ant. Interesting. He had never considered that his little trick could ever actually affect the universe, and that he could actually move time backwards.

He decided to try a little experiment. He turned on the television, and tuned it to his streaming service. He began a movie, and, watching it for a while, he noted where the film was in its story. Then he turned the audio off, so that only the picture was on, and there would be no dialogue in the background to distract him. He stared at his watch for a full five minutes this time, and then turned his attention back to the television. He could see it immediately in the video, but he resumed the audio just to confirm it. The movie was repeating scenes he has observed just five minutes before.

Was it him, or was his watch somehow imbued with the power to reverse time itself? He had a wind-up alarm clock, one that had fallen into disuse right after he had bought it, because he had quickly discovered the ticking kept him awake at night. He wound it up, and set it on the table in front of him. He never even bothered to set it to the correct time. Its second hand, spring-driven, advanced forward one numeral with each tick. And then, he concentrated.

His watch was battery driven, and, apparently, reversing the flow of electrons was easier than working against a mechanical spring. He found himself breaking out in a sweat, and concentrating harder than he ever had before. Finally, the second hand began moving backwards, one step at a time for each tick.

His bout with the alarm clock had yielded a dividend, however. With the watch, he had been able to march back a second in time for every number gained, as the second hand swept past. In other words, his time of concentration matched the time marched backwards. By increasing his level of concentration to that required by the alarm clock, however, he discovered he could make the second hand on the watch sweep backward ever more quickly.

In time, he was able to put the second hand into a slow backward spin, and the minute hand would move backward five minutes fairly quickly. But the really remarkable thing was, no matter how many times he did it, that the entire universe appeared to have marched backward in time as well.

Of course, these bouts of such extreme concentration were exhausting, and he could perform them over any length of time for just so long, and only so many times, before he required prolonged periods of rest.

But now that he had this power, what to do with it? At this point, he could only push the world an hour or so back in time. He could, he reasoned, possibly observe the rise of a stock price over an hour, push time back that hour, then place an electronic order at the old price, and sell the stock after the hour again passed—at the new, higher price. Of course, that would probably be immoral. But what if it could actually be done?

Just to amuse himself, he ran through the process a couple of times "just to test out the theory." It seemed to work: one stock advanced three points over an hour of trading, another one by five points. In the case of the first stock, buying a thousand dollars' worth of stock at the beginning of the hour would net two thousand dollars; the second stock would net four thousand. Of course, he would have to open an electronic trading account, have enough seed money in the account to allow him to begin trading, and pay a minimal fee for each transaction. But he was a poor man, and did not have the seed money.

He told himself that it would be wrong to exploit this new gift for personal gain, anyway, and set the idea aside — at least for the moment.

He *could* possibly do some good with his power: observe some disaster, for example, then move time backward sufficiently to give warning, thereby averting the disaster. What if, on September 11, 2001, he had observed the first jet flying into the north tower of the World Trade Center in New York on television, and then reversed time for an hour. But who would've listened to his warning in sufficient time to act on it? Who would he have even called, anyway? No, he was thinking too big. Perhaps if it was a smaller disaster? Say a traffic accident, or a house fire.

He knew a particular intersection to be dangerous. There had been several accidents there over the past several weeks. So, he found a perch at that corner and observed. Three days into his vigil, something finally happened: he observed an accident, and a bad one. An elderly woman crossing the intersection against the traffic light was struck by a car and was killed.

He stared at his watch. He didn't need to reverse time for an hour; fifteen minutes would be more than sufficient. He closed out all the noise around him, concentrating hard. The minute hand swept slowly backward — five, ten, fifteen minutes. When he lifted his head, everything was as it had been fifteen minutes earlier. When the old woman approached the intersection, and began to make her way across the street against the light, he grabbed her and pulled her backwards. "Don't!" he shouted. "The light is against you. You'll get hit by a car!" The old woman responded by swinging her handbag around her body and hitting him with it, square in the head.

"Let go," she shouted, and when he did, she proceeded into the crosswalk, and was struck by an oncoming car and killed. He was dumbstruck. Anyone observing might well conclude that instead of preventing the accident, he had caused it. Lest anyone come to that conclusion, he fled the scene.

TWO WEEKS LATER, HAVING FIRST gotten a high-interest loan for the seed money, he began investing in the market. He paid the loan off quickly, and within a month, was on his way to a modest fortune.

Gene Masters

Survival

As Irtuk left the snow-covered hut that morning, replacing the skins that sealed its interior from the frigid outside air, he knew that his hunt that day must be successful, or he and the family he just sealed inside his hut might well die.

It had been four days now since he had brought home so much as a fish to eat, and now he and his family had run out of food. It had been a woefully short summer, and the fields had produced far fewer tubers than normal, and practically no beans, nor grains. Even the seal oil the lamp burned to provide light was running out. It had been a long, hard winter, and spring was still at least two moons away. Without food soon, Irtuk and his family would not see the spring.

The edge of the ice pack was a good mile and a half from the hut. He picked up his harpoon, and, dragging his *umiak*—an open boat made of sealskin over a bone frame—behind him, began the trek to the sea. Fishing line, a supply of bone hooks, and his cast net for bait fish, were all stowed in the *umiak*. The weather was cold and damp, but, thankfully, there was no real wind, only a gentle icy breeze. The sun was still below the horizon. Its meager light would, in any case, be obscured by banks of gray clouds during its three-hour appearance this time of year. As he reached the edge of the ice, Irtuk surveyed the sea beyond. The surface was calm, with a few ripples.

There were none of the whitecaps that were normally stirred up by even a slightly strong wind.

Irtuk had set out four lines the evening before, before it got too dark to tend them. The first thing he did when he arrived, then, was to check them. The first three had caught nothing; a tug on each line showed the bait still intact. But the fourth line tugged back; there was at least one fish on it. He pulled the line in to see what had taken his hook during the night. As he retrieved his line, a grey head with bright eyes and a long-whiskered snout — a fur seal — emerged from the water about a hundred feet offshore. Seeing it, Irtuk pulled harder on the line. The head disappeared, and the water showed a rippling wake, as the seal swiftly made to steal Irtuk's catch. The fish had just broken the surface, and Irtuk scrambled, hand over hand, to retrieve his line. It was a nice salmon, plenty big enough to hold off his family's starvation for at least another day. But he could not bring in the line quickly enough. As fast as he was, the seal was faster, and the seal swallowed the salmon whole, taking fish, line, hook, and all.

Irtuk held onto the line for all he was worth. He was a squat man, built thick, and close to the ground; he was a man equipped with powerful arms and stout legs. The seal could have bitten down and severed the line, but it did not. The fish, Irtuk reasoned, must have stuck in its throat. Now, instead of just a salmon, Irtuk was wrestling with a fur seal at the end of his line.

The seal, Irtuk thought, had to be a female or a juvenile. There was no way even someone as strong as he was could wrestle a full-sized male from the shoreline.

As it was, he had to let out enough line to play the seal, or break the line, which he himself had woven from the long lengths of wire-sedge, that previous summer.

The seal's head emerged again from the water, the fishing line hanging from its partly-open mouth. It tried to bark back at Irtuk in defiance, but could manage only a feeble croak. It shook its head, trying to shake off the line, but it held fast. Then it dove again, pulling line with it, as Irtuk let line play out. When it stopped, Irtuk began to pull line back in. The seal, tired, allowed itself to be brought in, but only for a time. Once rested, it again surfaced, this time rising high out of the water, and, like a big fish, shook its head, trying to shake free, before it fell back into the sea and again disappeared below.

Irtuk was too busy concentrating on his fight with the seal to notice the arrival on the scene of yet another player. The drama had attracted the attention of a yearling orca, a killer whale, and seals were an orca's favorite prey. Here was a seal in trouble, not paying attention, and it should be easy pickings.

But the seal had somehow smelled this newest enemy, one, it calculated, that was far more dangerous than the enemy ashore. It flopped up and over the edge of the ice pack not twenty feet away from Irtuk, and only then did Irtuk see the black-and-white orca, with its mouth wide open, lunge out of the water after the retreating seal. It just missed biting down on the fleeing mammal's rear flippers. The orca, thwarted, sank back into the sea, and began swimming in a tight circle, in the hope, perhaps, that the seal might soon reenter the water.

But, now ashore, and walking erect and defiant on its four flippers, the seal faced off against Irtuk. Not questioning his luck, Irtuk rapidly picked up his harpoon, and quickly covering the distance between them, struck the seal a roundhouse blow on the head. The seal reeled, but did not go down, and Irtuk struck it again. This time, the seal did go down, and Irtuk buried the point of his harpoon in the animal's chest. With a dying gasp, the seal coughed up the salmon — hook, line, and all.

Irtuk was jubilant. The seal, he saw, was a young male, every bit as big as Irtuk himself. Here was enough meat, that, if cured properly, would last him and his family almost until spring. Irtuk smiled at his good fortune. He even had a nice salmon, besides.

It took him a while to load the seal (and the fish) onto the *umiak*. He rechecked his lines. As before, the first three were empty, the lines intact. Irtuk then reset the fourth line. Picking up his harpoon, he rinsed off the seal's blood in the sea, and then began dragging his *umiak* back to the hut.

THE BEAR STOOD UP AND sniffed at the cold breeze. There was a smell of fresh blood in the air. Something was dead or wounded, and the bear hadn't eaten in a while. The juvenile male had been on his own since the fall. The winter had been bitter, and it had been cold and dark in the den, so he had left the den weeks early. Now his body was craving fresh meat, and there was some close by. He could smell it. Walking on all fours, with a bear's peculiar gait — steady and lumbering, its front paws pigeon-towed — the bear followed the scent.

When the bear came upon Irtuk dragging his seal-laden *umiak* to the hut, both the bear and Irtuk reacted in surprise. Irtuk turned to the bear and braced, knees bent, bringing his harpoon up to the ready — a meager defense against an animal this size. In turn, the bear rose up on its hind legs, its stance wide, forepaws splayed wide, snarling, and showing white, sharp teeth.

The two adversaries stood, facing each other defiantly; neither, apparently, particularly eager to make the first move. The bear snarled and shook its head side to side, while Irtuk shouted out his defiance, brandishing his harpoon at the bear. This went on for some time.

Finally, the bear sidestepped Irtuk, and made for the *umiak* and fresh seal meat. Irtuk countered, lunging his harpoon forward at the bear, striking for his head, but missing, and instead piercing its right forepaw. The bear reared back again in fury, stared at its bleeding forepaw, and then lunged at Irtuk. Irtuk could do nothing other than aim the carved-bone point of his harpoon at the bear's chest, and plant its wooden shank in the snow. As Irtuk crouched and held on to his weapon for all his worth, the bear impaled himself on the harpoon.

Bear and harpoon clattered to one side, as Irtuk threw himself to the other. He almost escaped. The bear, still apparently writhing in his death throes, had trapped the bottom of Irtuk's left leg under its bulk.

When the bear was finally still, Irtuk attempted to pull his leg free, but to no avail. The beast was just too heavy, Irtuk's leg too firmly trapped in the snow beneath the bear. Now what to do? Irtuk looked up into the sky. The sun was just past its low-in-the-sky appearance, and it would soon be fully dark again. Irtuk had to somehow extract his leg from under the bear, and soon.

For the next half-hour or so, try as he might, he could not work his leg free. The bear was just too heavy, the snow packed too tight. Tired, he leaned back and rested for a while. If he could not get free, and if he was trapped there overnight, Irtuk knew he would probably freeze to death. He was almost reconciled to that fact, when the bear stirred.

The awakening bear put Irtuk into sheer panic. There was no telling how the wounded animal might react, and for Irtuk, trapped as he was, there was no possibility of retreat. He could do nothing but await his fate—whatever that might be. His only weapon, his harpoon, had landed on the other side of the animal when the bear fell, and was far out of reach.

The waking bear moved its right forepaw up to its muzzle, and groaned as it examined its pierced palm. It then placed the wounded palm against the bloody hole in its chest and groaned again, but louder. Finally, it rolled to its right and went into a fetal position, bringing its legs up into its wounded chest, and wrapping its arms around its body, and, in the process, freeing Irtuk's leg. (Later, Irtuk would swear that he then heard a mewling sound of the bear crying.)

Irtuk moved away from the bear, slowly and carefully, dragging himself along in the snow, until he felt it was safe for him to attempt to stand. When he finally did stand, his legs were wobbly, particularly the left one, which felt as if it had been carved from wood. He moved slowly and carefully, still backing away from the bear, until the feeling gradually returned to his left leg. Meanwhile, the bear was still curled up on its side, still making that mewling sound, still not moving.

The *umiak* and its precious cargo was still close by the bear. Irtuk considered leaving it, and making for home while there was sufficient daylight to safely do so. But, in his heart, he knew he could not. He had bested a killer whale and fought a bear for that seal meat, and now he could not leave it behind. Slowly, cautiously, he approached the place where the *umiak's* hauling rope lay in a jumbled heap on the snow, careful to keep the *umiak* between himself and the bear. Still, the bear did not move.

Picking up the hauling rope, he pulled on it, moving it from side to side, until the *umiak* was free and began to slide. Irtuk then thought to put distance between himself and the fallen bear. But he could not. His curiosity was far too powerful, and the wounded bear far too much of a source of wonder. Why had the animal, upon awakening, not lashed out at the cause of its misery and mauled him? What was Irtuk to make of the animal now: a poor, pathetic ball of fur, just lying in the snow, making that pitiful sound?

Irtuk told himself he must now approach the bear to retrieve his harpoon, still lying next to the animal. And so, he did. Standing next to the bear, Irtuk looked down, and the bear looked up at Irtuk. When their eyes met, Irtuk could feel the animal's pain. Leaving the harpoon, he went back to the *umiak*, and picking up the salmon, then returned and laid it on the snow next to the bear.

Then Irtuk again picked up the haul rope and dragged the *umiak* back to his hut and waiting family.

EARLY THE FOLLOWING MORNING, IRTUK went back out to check his fishing lines, and on the way found the place where he had left his harpoon. It was still there, but the bear was gone. And so was the salmon.

The Night Visitor

It was the dead of night, and I was sound asleep, and I thought that perhaps I was still dreaming.

"You're not dreaming," the pretty little girl next to my bed said to me. "You are very much awake."

"How could I be?" I asked. "You can't be real. The house is locked up tight—I know it is—and there is no way you could be here, not really. And while you are quite beautiful, all sparkling and blue-eyed, and all dressed up in that frilly yellow dress, I'm afraid you're nothing more than a bit of undigested pork, or perhaps that glass of bad wine."

She laughed, and even her laugh sparkled. It was only then that I noticed that while it was pitch black outside my window, my bedroom was lit with a pleasant glow, and its source seemed to be my visitor.

"Am I real now?" she asked. "Will you give me your hand?"

I took my arm out from beneath the covers and extended my hand. She took it in hers, and her little hand was solid enough, the flesh warm. "So, now, does my hand feel like a bit of undigested pork?" she asked.

"Of course not. But if you are a part of an elaborate dream, your hand would feel quite real, after all, wouldn't it?"

She frowned, her face pretty even as she frowned. "Very well." She paused, and then said, "When you do dream, and feel threatened, have you ever tried to shout out loud?"

"Yes."

"And were you able to shout out—out loud, that is?"

"No, I could not."

"And what happened after that?"

"Well, I reasoned that I was dreaming, and woke up."

"Exactly. We are alone in the house. Go ahead and shout. If you are dreaming, then you will awake and I will disappear. Go ahead and shout!"

And I did. I let out a bellow. The sound came from out of my body with ease, and were I still asleep, I knew, I could have managed only a whimper. And my visitor was still there. And she giggled a little girl giggle.

"See?" she said, delight lighting up her face. "You're not dreaming. I *am* here, and I *am* real."

"But that's not possible," I said, quite sure that even if I were awake, she existed only in my mind. "I'm hallucinating."

She frowned again. "First, I'm a bit of pork, and now I'm a figment of your imagination. What must I do to convince you that I am real?"

"I have no idea," I said and thought for a bit. "Perhaps if you told me who you are, how you got in here, and why you're here to begin with?"

"Oh, dear," she said, "I'm afraid that if I do explain all of that, you will be even more certain that you're imagining me."

Now it was my turn to smile. I sat up in bed. "Humor me," I said.

"Very well. Tell me, George, do you believe in the spiritual?"

"I believe in God, if that's what you mean. Say, how do you know my name?"

"The Master knew your name even before you were in your mother's womb, and he told me your name."

"The Master?"

"Yes. It is he whom I follow."

I digested that bit of information for a bit, and then said, "Go on."

"I asked if you believed in the spiritual, and you said that you believed in God. Of course, God is a spirit, but what of others? Do you believe that all of mankind have spiritual souls? That in addition to humans, God created pure spiritual beings that humans call angels?"

"I am not at all sure about all of that. I believed in all of those things when I was your age, but as I grew older I became a little more skeptical."

"Well then, you're not going to like the answer to the rest of your questions. As to who I am, I don't have a name exactly, but I am a spirit—an angel to be exact . . ."

I made to protest, raising my hand, palm out, a "stop there" motion.

"Hear me out!" she insisted. "There will be time enough for your negativity after I've finished!" Somehow, she now seemed a trifle older than I first assumed her to be.

"Very well," I relented. "Carry on."

"I am, as I said," she continued, "an angel. Since I am an angel, how I got here is obvious. Physical boundaries pose no barriers for me. Why I am here is simply this—my Master has sent me to claim your soul."

I have to admit that that comment threw me. This child had just told me that I would die this night, hadn't she? But, before voicing my objections to what she had just said, I decided to leave that for the moment and try a different tack.

"Very well, then, if you are an angel, then you are a pure spirit. Yet you spent a great deal of effort earlier to convince me that you were not a dream, but a material being. I held your hand in my own. You are flesh and blood."

"I am, but just for the moment. I must take on a physical presence for you to see me and converse with me directly." She saw my look and paused. "Come now, I know you're familiar with the Bible. It is full of instances with angels appearing to people. We are messengers, after all. How am I supposed to give you a message if you can't see me or hear me?"

"All right, if I give you that, then why appear as a little girl?"

"Would you have stayed in bed and listened to me if I showed up as a monster? As I am, I clearly pose no threat, and, besides, an apparition this size requires a lot less matter be gathered." But even as she said that, I saw that her body had begun to mature. She was no longer a little girl; she was growing up before my eyes.

"Very well, then. But you say you're here after my soul? For your Master? Who exactly is this Master of yours, and why would I give him my soul?"

"You misunderstood me. I said I am here to *claim* your soul. You have already givin it to him, have you not?"

"Have I? How do you figure? And is your Master who I think he is?"

"You have indeed, and you *do* already know my Master. You have worshipped him, just as I always have and always will."

Now I was uncomfortable. "We're talking the Devil here, aren't we—Satan, Lucifer, Beelzebub, Asmodeus, right?"

"Well, yes," she said, now having blossomed into a lovely young woman, "generally speaking. Although Beelzebub and Asmodeus are actually just lesser demons—important, mind you, but not up to the level of the chief." Her little-girl dress was gone, and she now wore a "simple black dress," one which complimented her womanly curves.

"And I've already willed your Master my soul?"

"You have." From somewhere she produced an apple. It was red and ripe, and filled the bedroom with its apple-cider aroma. "You have, and you have already eaten of the forbidden fruit." She took a bite out of the apple, and then set it on the nightstand. "You have shared in the legacy of the Master. He and the angels that followed him—I among them—were driven from paradise, because he thought himself the equal of God.

"He brought death into the world because he convinced your first ancestors that partaking of forbidden fruit would make them like God. And now you, George, knowing of God, have convinced yourself that you are his equal by substituting your own will for his. So how are you not just like my Master?"

And for that I had no answer. I lay there, and was ashamed, for even as I lay accused of a life consumed in self-absorption, I felt a sudden lustful urging for this beautiful creature standing before me. "And am I to die, tonight then? Is my soul to separate from my body tonight, so that you may claim it for your Master? Take me then."

"Not tonight, George, but soon, very soon. Oh, make no mistake, I would take you tonight if it was possible, but even the Master cannot, in the end, thwart the will of God. And God has willed that you are not to die yet, not tonight."

I felt as if a great weight had suddenly been lifted from my body. "What then?" I asked.

"Return to sleep," she said, and touched my face, sweeping her hand down over my eyes, which closed in a deep, refreshing sleep.

I awoke the next morning, somehow sitting up in bed, yet relaxed and refreshed from sleep as I had not been for some time previous. *What a strange dream,* I mused, shrugging it off. *If dreams have any meaning, I wonder what brought that one on. No matter,* my musings continued, *I'm far too old to change my ways at this juncture.*

Then, on my nightstand, I saw the apple—red and ripe, with one bite taken out of it.

The Cavern

Og had been getting away with stealing his neighbor Gilbod's chickens for several weeks. Then Og was caught red-handed in Gilbod's chicken house; Gilbod and his neighbor Zaug, caught him there, holding a squawking bird by its feet.

No defense that Og could come up with satisfied the Council of Twelve, and Og was sentenced to the cavern. When proffered the sleeping potion by the bailiff, Og obstinately refused to drink. So, four men held Og down, while the bailiff poured the potion down his throat.

WHEN OG AWOKE, HE WAS in the cavern. The place was lit by the efflorescent lichen that lived on its ceiling and walls, but it still took a few minutes for Og to adapt to the cavern's low light level. When his eyes did adjust to the eerie greenish glow, Og looked all around, scanning his prison. The cavern, he noted, was big. Very big. There were efflorescent-coated outcroppings of sold stone in the continuous, enveloping wall, with crevices and niches, and here and there dark holes: tunnels leading into, and out of, the place.

"So, you are awake," a voice came from out of the depths. Og searched in the direction of the voice. Then, there, emerging from the green haze, was a human form.

"Who are you?" Og asked, taking a defensive stance.

"I am Sihan," the form responded, "condemned to this place, apparently, just as you are. But do not mind me. I mean you no harm, nor could I inflict it, were I so minded."

Og could make him out clearly now: a slight man, thin and hairy, his tattered skin hanging loose on a spare frame. "I am Og," he said, "son of Og, and of the tribe of the Bashan."

"As am I," Sihan said, "son of Crates, and also of the tribe of the Bashan."

"I never saw you. But, then, we Bashan occupy a large territory."

"That we do," Sihan pridefully agreed.

"You have been here since a long time?"

"I have, but cannot say how long. But I would wager for several moons — or, at least, so it has seemed," Sihan responded.

"And there are others in here besides you?"

"Not now. But there have been others. Each has tried his luck finding a way back to the surface. Each has disappeared into one of the tunnels. None has ever returned. But I know not if any has escaped. Have you heard?"

"I have not," Og admitted, "But then I have never made such an enquiry."

"Ah," Sihan sighed, "I had so hoped. Anyone who makes it back to the surface, you know, is declared innocent of the crime that put him here."

"I did, but never expected to be caught and put in here in the first place. But I am hungry. What do you eat?"

"In the pools, scattered along the base of the cavern wall, live creatures of jellied flesh. A fish of sorts, I think. Grasping them is a trick learned by trial and error. They are tasteless, but sustain life. There are enough in here to sustain one man, but, when there are two or more, then only barely. Are you planning to stay for long, or will you try your luck in the tunnels?"

But Og did not answer Sihan. Instead, he was busily inching his way toward the cavern wall, in search of such a pool. When he reached the wall, he reached out and touched it, only to have some lichen adhere to his fingers, outlining his fingers in a green glow. He turned and continued his slow pace, now making his way along the wall. Then he almost stepped into one of the pools.

"Careful," Sihan warned, suddenly beside him. "The pools are deep," he warned, "and the water like ice. It is cold enough in here without falling in and getting wet."

"The water," Og asked, "good to drink, is it?"

"It must be," Sihan replied, "else I would be dead."

"Of course," Og admitted. Then, kneeling, took a long drink. "It tastes and smells of brimstone," he noted, and drank again. Then he reached deep into the pool, searching for a jellyfish. Several skittered past his glowing fingers, but he could not catch them.

"The glow is good," Sihan said, "and it does attract them. But you must be quicker."

Sihan rubbed his hand on the wall, and when his fingers glowed like Og's, he knelt and dipped into the pool. Seconds later he withdrew a gelatinous wriggling mass and sucked it down his throat. He withdrew another, and, cupping it in both hands, offered it to Og.

Og took it, brought it to his mouth, and swallowed it down.

"Like eating snot," he said. "and, thankfully, as you said, tasteless."

"You eat it if you wish to live," Sihan said dejectedly.

OG SURVIVED THROUGH SEVERAL SUCH meals, sleeping at those times when he felt sleepy. He could only assume that his interior clock was marking off the days. It soon became evident to him, that, unlike his complacent cavern companion, he must seek a way out, and make it back to the surface—or die trying.

"When they brought me here, Sihan, did you notice the tunnel from whence they emerged?"

"I did."

"And?"

"And, when you were still asleep, I entered it. But the tunnel walls have no lichen, and they are pitch black. I went in a way, feeling my way along in the dark, and then the one tunnel became two. I chose one, and went farther, only to come to another such fork. I lost my nerve and made my way back here again."

"And can you tell which tunnel that was now?"

"I cannot. I should have marked it, but I did not."

"Yes, you should have," Og agreed.

Og reflected on that narration for another two sleepings, before he settled on an escape plan.

"WHAT ARE YOU DOING?" SIHAN ASKED.

"Getting ready to leave this place," Og replied, "You can come with me if you like."

"I will not. I do not wish to die of hunger and thirst, lost in some dark tunnel."

"Of hunger and thirst possibly, but not in the dark."

"How so?"

"Watch and learn," Og answered.

As Sihan watched, Og went to the cavern wall and began to fish in one of the pools. He had long since become proficient at grabbing the jellyfish and proceeded to gorge on them. When he ate all he could hold, he began to drink, but his stomach was full, and he could not drink very much.

"Stocking up on food and water while you can," Sihan observed.

Without answering, Og stood and began smearing his body with lichen. When he had covered himself completely, he picked up the flattest rock he could find, and heaped as much lichen on it as it would hold.

"Making a torch of yourself. Brilliant!" Sihan observed. "You will have light in the tunnels. But why the lichen on the rock?"

"Come with me and you shall see," Og said. "Are you sure you do not wish to come with me now?"

"I am," Sihan replied, somewhat sadly. "Life here is monotonous, but it is life nonetheless. But I will miss you, Og, and I wish you good fortune."

Og only grunted an acknowledgement, and made for the nearest tunnel.

"Why *that* tunnel?" Sihan asked, now a disembodied voice in a greenish void.

"No reason. It seems as good as any other."

And with that, Og started his journey forward, carrying his flat rock, his very body a torch to light his way. Sihan watched as his late companion disappeared into the tunnel, the light fading quickly, as Og moved away. Soon, the light was gone.

It was not long before Og came to a fork. He looked at the floor of each of the two new tunnels, but neither appeared to be rising upward. Taking a smear of lichen from the flat rock, Og smeared some lichen on the wall of the right tunnel and arbitrarily took that route forward. He had not traveled much farther when the same thing happened, and again Og ended up choosing the rightmost tunnel. Another smear on the wall, and he again moved forward.

It was in this last tunnel that Og stumbled upon his first corpse. It could not have been there too long, since there was still some flesh attached to the bones. Og pictured the man stumbling about in the dark, feeling his way along, inching his way ever forward. Finally, the poor fool's stamina must have run out, and he just laid down and died.

Then occurred what he had feared most. He came to another fork. On the rightmost tunnel wall was a greenish glow from the lichen he had smeared there earlier. He had traveled in a circle, and he did not know if this was the first or second set of forks he had encountered. Perhaps the dead man he had just passed in the tunnel had done just that: had traveled around in this same circle until his time ran out. But now Og had

100

no choice but to smear the wall on the tunnel to the left, and try that route.

As he traveled along this tunnel, it had several tunnels entering into it from the side, both off Og's left and his right. He chose to ignore these, and stuck to the main tunnel, continuing forward. He had no sensation of going either up or down in elevation, and that worried him. *I might never find a route leading up to the surface.*

Again, a fork, one large tunnel leading to the left, a much smaller one to the right. Smearing the wall of the leftmost, he took it, and had not gone very far when it opened into a large cavern. It was not nearly as large as the original prison cavern, and lacked the fluorescent lichen. But in its center, he found a large pool. Og tasted its water, and it tasted much like the brimstone water of the prison cavern, so he drank his fill. He felt for some jellyfish but found none. *At least I will not die of thirst.*

He realized that he was tired, counted his time spent in the tunnels thus far as a full day, and laid down to sleep next to the pool.

Upon awakening, Og got up and surveyed this new cavern. The floor seemed relatively flat, and the walls had crags and outcropping much like the prison cavern. It was while exploring the cavern, that he ran across two more bodies, each a pile of bones at the base of the cavern wall, but on opposite sides.

Then he counted five exit tunnels, all pretty much the same size, including the one he had come from. But now he did not know which one that was.

Drinking deep from the pool, and shrugging off his feeling of stupidity for not marking the tunnel he had come from, he chose one of the tunnels at random. He marked the entryway, and went forward. He again kicked himself for a fool when he came upon the smear on the wall he had made the day before.

Backtracking, he reentered the second cavern. Then he chose another tunnel, marked its wall, and moved forward. He walked for a while, passing up a side tunnel, continuing forward until the main tunnel ended abruptly in a blank wall. He backtracked, and, marking it, took the first side tunnel. Only, a short time later, he found himself back in the second cavern, two of its tunnels marked with lichen. This time, he marked the wall of the tunnel he had just exited. Now three of the five tunnels into the cavern led, he knew, nowhere. There were just two remaining. He took the one on the left, smearing its wall.

As he advanced in this new tunnel, he noted that the lichen he had smeared on his body had lost most of its efflorescence. The lichen he carried on the flat rock had not, but now there was much less of it left than when he has started out. He had been generous in smearing the tunnel entrances; now he must conserve what he had left, since he feared it may eventually become his only source of light.

He was not very far along in the tunnel when he passed yet another pile of bones. These looked (as well as he could see in the now very dim light) as if they had been there for some time. He wondered how many other bodies may have been deposited in those tunnels he had passed up and had not traveled.

With this last tunnel, he had a feeling that the cave floor beneath him was rising, and it was. But so also was the tunnel roof falling. The tunnel's floor, ceiling, and walls were closing in. Soon he could not advance without stooping. The stooping became a frog walk, and then a crawl. Og thought about turning back, but something urged him forward. It was, he soon realized, a gentle draft he felt on his face. Pushing the flat rock forward in front of him, he crawled ever forward, as the cave's confines continued to close in on him.

Suddenly, with a last push forward, the flat rock disappeared from sight. He heard its clatter as it fell off into some space in front of him. *I must get it! It has all my light! I must get it!* He squeezed forward, his head and body scraping on the tunnel's confines, when he barely emerged into some new space. On a floor, some distance bellow him, the scattered remnant of the spilled lichen glowed. But the light was insufficient. This new space was a space undefined in the dark. He squeezed forward into nothingness. Og had no other choice now, but to push on.

As he emerged from what was essentially just a hole, Og bent his body forward, arms extended, flattening himself against what had to be yet another cavern wall. The lichen-lit floor was still a foot or two below him when he emerged completely, and he fell those few feet, exhausted. As pulled himself into a sitting position against the wall, Og scanned the space in front of him, but beyond the immediate lichen glow, all was dark.

Falling into an exhausted sleep, Og imagined he could feel a strong draft on his face, and hear a faint whistling sound off in the distance.

When he awoke, Og was amazed to find the confines of the space he occupied to be now clearly defined, dimly lit like a new dawn. It was lit with a yellow, and not green, light. He was in yet another cavern, this one much smaller than the others, and what had to be daylight was entering from somewhere ahead.

But, save the lichen glow, it was black as night when I fell into this place. Why of course — it was black as night because it was night! *And now it is day!*

Getting up from his place against the cave wall, Og stretched, and then walked slowly to the light. He found it came from a shaft leading diagonally upward, a shaft just big enough, and flat enough, for a man to crawl through.

A few minutes later, Og emerged into the daylight. The morning air was crisp and clean, and a meadow below was bathed in gold by the risen Sun. He breathed in deep the breath of life, and basked in the bright warmth of freedom. Freedom and innocence.

About the Author

Gene Masters is a retired consulting engineer living in East Tennessee with his wife, Ruth. They have two grown daughters, and two grandchildren. He is the author of several technical treatises, including his doctoral dissertation, and seven novels.

Masters received a commission in the U.S. Navy on graduation from Notre Dame, and his first tour of duty was aboard a transport in the Western Pacific. His second tour was aboard a recommissioned and updated diesel-electric submarine, the USS *Angler*, which was originally commissioned in 1943, and made seven war patrols in the Pacific before being decommissioned. Her updating to an SSK-class boat in the 1950s fitted her for operation against cold war submarine adversaries with advanced soundproofing and sonar. Masters left *Angler* and active duty after a Mediterranean tour. Later Naval Reserve assignments included the diesel-electric submarines USS *Manta* and the USS *Ling*.

After active duty, Masters pursued a career in engineering, and served in various companies until settling into a career as a consulting engineer. He retired in 2009. Readers can reach the author via email at 240boat@gmail.com, and view his website at *www.genemasters.net*.

From the Author

I hope you have enjoyed *A Baker's Dozen*. While my primary intention was to entertain you with short stories that might fit neatly into niches in your daily schedule, I also had another thought in mind, that being to introduce you to my work and to pique your curiosity in my longer works.

To date, I have written eight novels, including four mysteries. All of them are available in print and in eBook format. I hope you will consider purchasing one or all of them. Here is a complete list, in the order they were written:

Silent Warriors: Submarine Warfare in the Pacific
Operation Exodus
The Laconia Incident
The Wounds of Jonas Clark

<u>Rich Vitelli Mysteries</u>
The Dry Cleaner
True Believers
Bobby Doyle is Missing
Vitelli in Venice

A Word About Reviews

Reviews are the lifeblood of any author. If you've enjoyed *A Baker's Dozen*, I hope you will please consider writing a brief review and posting it wherever you think it might be of some help.

Thanks in advance!

Gene Masters

www.ingramcontent.com/pod-product-compliance
Lightning Source LLC
Chambersburg PA
CBHW030551130626
46552CB00006B/2500